# BEYOND SEVEN FORESTS

# BEYOND SEVEN FORESTS

AMANDA McCRINA

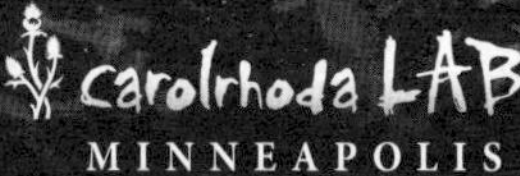

carolrhoda LAB
MINNEAPOLIS

Carolrhoda Lab®
An imprint of Lerner Publishing Group, Inc.
241 First Avenue North
Minneapolis, MN 55401 USA

For reading levels and more information, look up this title at www.lernerbooks.com.

Map by Laura K. Westlund.

Design elements: Mandrysz Krzysztof/Shutterstock; SaveJungle/Shutterstock; Improviser/Shutterstock; railway fx/Shutterstock; PawelG Photo/Shutterstock; mycola/Getty Images; ngraphix1/Shutterstock.

Main body text set in Minion Pro.
Typeface provided by Adobe Systems.

**Library of Congress Cataloging-in-Publication Data**

Names: McCrina, Amanda, 1990– author.
Title: Beyond seven forests / Amanda McCrina.
Description: Minneapolis : Carolrhoda Lab, 2026. | Audience term: Teenagers | Audience: Ages 14–18. | Audience: Grades 10–12. | Summary: "In 1916, amidst World War I, a blizzard traps eighteen-year-old Polish countess Renata in her home with two Polish deserters from the Russian army"— Provided by publisher.
Identifiers: LCCN 2025005710 | ISBN 9798765670811 (library binding) | ISBN 9798765691533 (epub)
Subjects: CYAC: World War, 1914–1918—Fiction. | Countesses—Fiction. | Soldiers—Fiction. | Polish people—Fiction. | Russians—Poland—Fiction. | LCGFT: Historical fiction. | Novels.
Classification: LCC PZ7.1.M4334 Be 2026 | DDC [Fic]—dc23

LC record available at https://lccn.loc.gov/2025005710

Manufactured in Guang Dong, China by Dream Colour Printing
1-1012709-54100-6/9/2025

**In memory of**
**Tomasz Marcin Sękala**
**2001–2024**
**Oddał swoje życie za wolność**

# NOTE TO READERS

Parts of this story deal with sexual violence, PTSD, and suicide. For 24/7 free and confidential support and resources, these are some places to start.

Suicide & Crisis Lifeline: call or text 988

National Sexual Assault Hotline: call 800-656-4673 or use the online chat at https://hotline.rainn.org/online

National Mental Health Hotline: call 866-903-3787

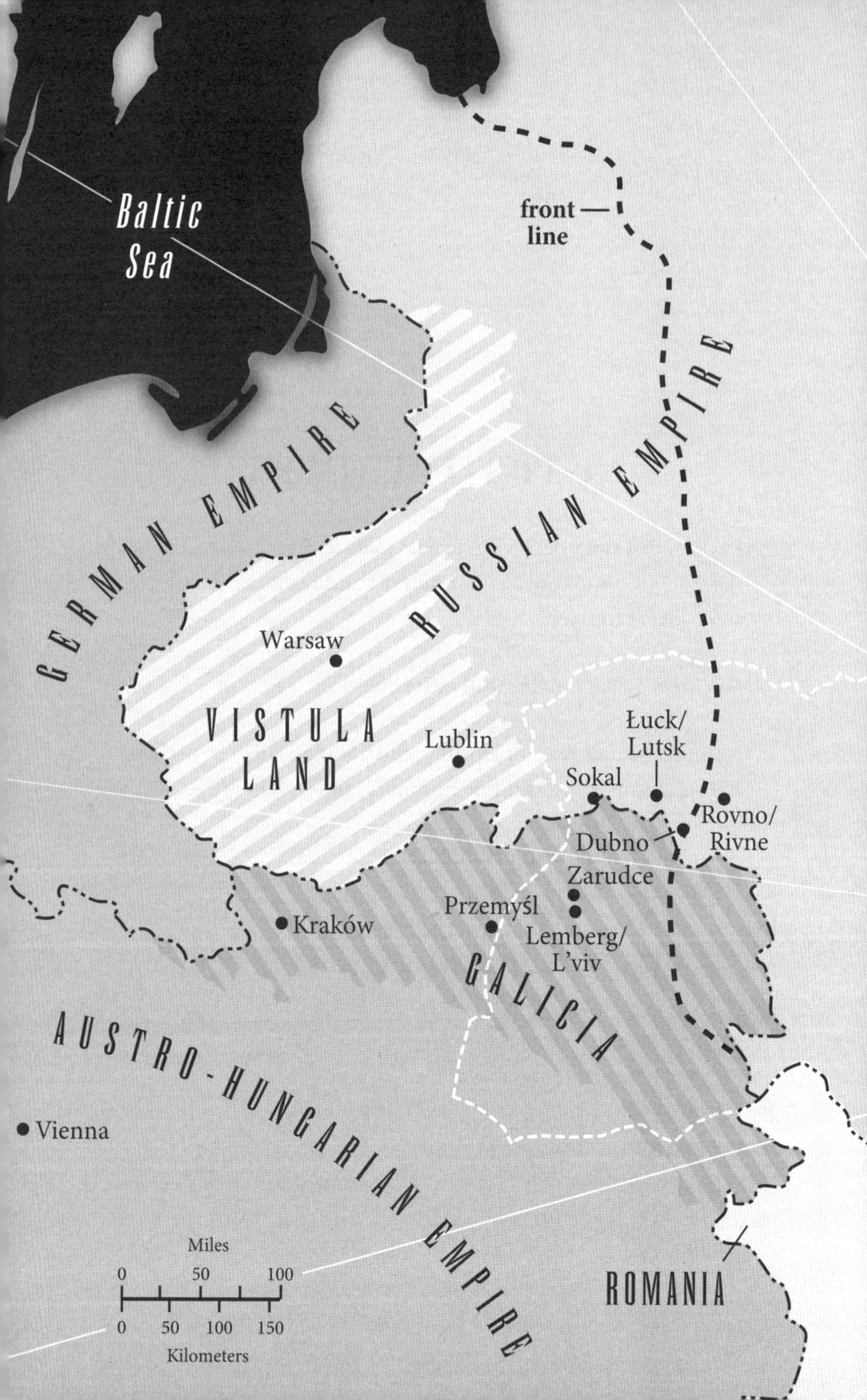

Baltic Sea
front line
GERMAN EMPIRE
RUSSIAN EMPIRE
Warsaw
VISTULA LAND
Lublin
Łuck/ Lutsk
Sokal
Rovno/ Rivne
Dubno
Zarudce
Przemyśl
Kraków
Lemberg/ L'viv
GALICIA
AUSTRO-HUNGARIAN EMPIRE
Vienna
Miles
0 50 100
0 50 100 150
Kilometers
ROMANIA

# World War I Eastern Front, 1916

front line, early summer 1916
national border, 1916
Ukraine border, 21st century
city

RUSSIAN EMPIRE

Kyiv

N
E
W
S

Black Sea

# PRELUDE

Beyond seven mountains, beyond seven forests . . .

That's how all the old stories begin. *Za siedmioma górami, za siedmioma lasami.* Sometimes the storyteller will say instead, "Beyond seven mountains, beyond seven seas . . ." but my father always said *lasami*, forests. Perhaps because our house sat right at the brink of the wild old forest above Lemberg, and that brought the stories closer to home. Neither Mieszko nor I had ever seen the sea.

So this is how my story begins: beyond seven mountains, beyond seven forests, in the dead of winter, in the third year of the war.

# CHAPTER 1

## FRIDAY, JANUARY 7, 1916
## GALICIA, AUSTRO-HUNGARIAN EMPIRE

My courtroom is not a courtroom. It is the parlor of the manor house on the old Potocki estate just outside Lemberg. I've taken tea in this parlor many times, though not since before the war. There was some discussion, five or six years ago, of a possible match between the younger Count Potocki and myself, until he lost his life in a motorcar race in France. The elder Count Potocki paid protection money to the Russians, so the house and grounds remained mostly untouched during the occupation and then the retreat last summer.

It didn't do him any good in the end. The Austrians hanged him as a collaborator in July. They hanged a great many people as collaborators in July.

In any case, this house is almost certainly the only szlachcic's house within thirty kilometers of Lemberg that still has four good walls and an intact roof. General von Linsingen, the German commander, has been using it as his headquarters all winter—and as the courtroom for his military tribunals, which is why I am here.

Most of those here this morning to witness my sentencing are officers of von Linsingen's staff, but they've brought in a small contingent from the Polish Legions to handle the questioning itself. An acknowledgment of my Polish title, I suppose, and of my status as an Austro-Hungarian subject, not a German one. The Legions answer to the Austro-Hungarian high command.

I recognize Commandant Piłsudski, their leader, though I've never met him. He and his staff arrived just last night from an inspection of the front lines, one hundred and fifty kilometers to the east. He is impossible not to recognize. He wears a theatrical full mustache, wider than his face, to hide—so the story goes—two missing front teeth, his souvenir from a Russian prison.

I have no jury. No one, I think, is in any suspense as to what the verdict will be. Captain Baran—poor jealous, aggrieved Captain Baran—has brought the charges. General von Linsingen will decide my sentence, and Commandant Piłsudski will pronounce it.

The firing squad, most likely: This is a military tribunal, and that is the usual manner of execution prescribed by military tribunals. I am lucky to have this tribunal at all. There was no such courtesy for Count Potocki. The hangings in July were summary ones.

I am not ignorant of the ways in which I am shielded by my status as a szlachcianka, a noblewoman. I am—to use my full name—Countess Renata Krystyna Zamoyska of the Jelita coat of arms, daughter of an ancient and powerful knightly family. A peasant accused of a crime such as mine would almost certainly not have her case tried before General von Linsingen himself. That is my privilege. It is, of course, far more honorable to die before a firing squad like a soldier than to hang like a common criminal.

As for defenders, I have only the one, and he will not be permitted to speak. He sits handcuffed and flanked by two German guards at the back of the room, cleaned up now, smooth-shaven and handsome, though his face is still swollen and purple in places from the beating he took four days ago at Captain Baran's hands. His Russian lieutenant's uniform is washed and neatly pressed. He couldn't speak even if they were to let him. General von Linsingen speaks neither Russian nor Polish, so on his orders—and with my permission, though I don't imagine I had the option to refuse—my trial has been conducted in German. But they have brought the lieutenant in to watch.

Captain Baran's doing? Or perhaps the lieutenant asked to be here, so I wouldn't be alone. It will be his turn before the tribunal as soon as they've finished with me. His sentence will very likely be the same as mine, though for a different charge.

There is a typist here, a junior officer of Commandant Piłsudski's staff, to record the proceedings. Commandant Piłsudski is taking a great deal of care to follow every protocol to the letter. There are whispers in the coffeehouses and salons and on the street corners of Lemberg that he means very soon to break with the Central Powers and declare an independent Polish republic, backed by his loyal legions. If he is to succeed at his state-building, he must succeed in convincing the world that he is the sort of person to do things considerately and properly—including, I suppose, the court-martial of one of his compatriots.

The typist feeds another leaf of paper into his machine. There's a stretch of busy silence as he turns knobs and pulls levers and makes adjustments.

The examining officer—an intelligent and painstakingly thorough young man introduced to me this morning as Lieutenant Colonel Sosnkowski—speaks to me. "Before we proceed to your sentencing, Countess Zamoyska"—they've all been very careful to use the proper titles and forms of address, made more difficult because everything must be translated into German—"is there anything you would like to say?"

It's an unexpected kindness on his part. There are rumors surrounding Colonel Sosnkowski too—that he is the commandant's right-hand man, his most trusted agent, the doer of his dirty work. That his intelligence operatives, the Organizacja Wojskowa, are active here in Lemberg and in liberated Russian Poland as well as at the front. That he is the one responsible for the mysterious deaths of a number of Russian officers behind their own lines. I had built him up to be rather a fearsome and dangerous figure in my head. But he is to all appearances a polite, unassuming young man with mild gray-blue eyes creased at the corners by laugh lines, and he has shown nothing but courtesy to me.

All the same, I have nothing else to say. I have no defense to make. He has already secured my confession.

There was some debate over what the exact charge should be. Collaboration? Aiding and comforting the enemy? I did aid two officers of the Imperial Russian army, it's true—escaped prisoners of war at that. But they were no longer active combatants. In fact, they'd ended up our prisoners in the first place because they'd deserted the Russian lines near Rovno. In any case, that wasn't why I was arrested four days ago.

They've settled on "actions deemed disruptive to the war effort" for reasons I don't dispute.

"Thank you, Colonel Sosnkowski," I tell him now. "There is nothing I would like to say."

"It would be helpful for us to have your account for the record."

"Captain Baran has presented the facts very clearly. I have no argument."

"Nevertheless," Colonel Sosnkowski persists, "for thoroughness's sake, we would like to hear your explanation."

"My explanation, Colonel?"

"If you please, Countess. We know what you did. We would like to know why."

It occurs to me that he's offering me the chance to win the court's pity. The chance, perhaps, to have my sentence commuted, should General von Linsingen find my side of the story compelling enough.

But I am not sure how much good it will do. It seems very clear to me that General von Linsingen—a jowly, bull-necked old soldier who keeps stealing glances at his wristwatch—considers the entire proceeding to be a waste of his time. I am the footnote here. Lieutenant Kijek, as an enemy officer, is of much more interest to General von Linsingen and of much more value to the war effort.

At any rate, I was brought up to spurn pity and to stand by my own actions unflinchingly, whatever their consequences may be.

As I am a service member of the military medical staff of the Austro-Hungarian Empire, however, and he is technically my superior officer, I feel obliged to comply.

"Very well," I say. "I will tell you why."

# CHAPTER 2

Where does one start to explain why one is a traitor?

I doubt anyone expected it of me. Our little Galician branch of the Zamoyski family—once one of the most powerful and important families in the Polish-Lithuanian Commonwealth, before the commonwealth's downfall and the dividing up of Poland among Russia, Prussia, and Austria a little more than a century ago—has long since proven its loyalty to the Habsburg crown. The men of the family have served dutifully in the Habsburg army. My grandfather, Count Stanisław Zamoyski, was in Bosnia with Baron von Philippsberg and earned the Merit Cross there.

But of course I am being tried for my actions, and my actions alone.

I imagine there are those who will blame it on my childhood or my upbringing and say that the signs were always there, that there was always some weakness of character manifest. And perhaps they are right. My brother, Mieszko, five years older than I, could've readily recounted any number of my weaknesses of character, I'm sure—though if you'd told him I would be standing before this tribunal today accused of disrupting the war effort, he might very well have laughed in your face. Captain Baran was a friend of his, but even so he'd be the first to tell you the captain must be mistaken in this case. I think he always saw me as rather overcautious and stickling. He was the reckless one.

My childhood and upbringing were, I think, fairly unremarkable altogether—that is, fairly typical for a young woman of my status and privilege. You all know my father's antecedents; my mother's family is equally distinguished, though her only living kin now are her cousins in England whom I've never met. I've lived the entirety of my eighteen years in Zarudce, in that same house in which I was arrested four days ago.

I took lessons in German, French, English, piano, flute, needlework, horseback riding, and social etiquette. Less typically, at my father's insistence, I learned to milk cows and to birth foals and to plan and plant a crop, though I don't believe this instilled any objectionable qualities in me.

I was betrothed at fourteen to the son of a prominent and respected Austrian noble family; I made my requisite appearance at the imperial court in Vienna at sixteen.

I was never headstrong or impetuous or outspoken or any of those things that are considered dashing in young men but unbecoming to young women. I rather prided myself on not being any of those things. I suppose that shows one weakness of character.

All this to say, I don't think anyone is more surprised at my turning traitor than I am.

I could start with young Captain Witkowski's wounded foot: If not for the boy's injury, the fugitives wouldn't have come to the house. Or I could start with the snowstorm: If not for the storm, they wouldn't have stayed long enough to cause further trouble. In either case, I would not be standing before this tribunal today.

But neither beginning would be the whole truth.

I think I must first go back to July of last year, when I watched the Austrians hang a boy.

I was coming home from the hospital in Lemberg, having just been discharged. They were hanging the boy from a linden tree just outside Zarudce, on that stretch of road that runs for a little while along the riverbank. They were soldiers of the Twelfth Infantry Division of the Austro-Hungarian Sixth Corps, which was then under Herr General Mackensen's command—

**"You seem to have a very detailed knowledge of the command structure, Countess," Colonel Sosnkowski says.**

**"Yes, Colonel. We are required at the hospital to make note of unit and commanding officer for each casualty. I can name most of the units of the Heeresgruppe, as at this point I've treated casualties from most of them."**

**"Ah, yes, you're a nurse."**

**"I am not a nurse." Pointless pride, but I can't help myself. "I am a doctor's assistant in the military medical service of the Austro-Hungarian Empire. Forgive me, Colonel, but I was under the impression that was why I am being tried before a military tribunal rather than before the Reichsgericht in Vienna."**

**"You are being tried before this tribunal because it is expedient, Countess, and because Herr General von Linsingen"—Colonel Sosnkowski inclines his head to the general in appropriate deference—"has generously afforded you the opportunity to have your case heard by your fellow Poles."**

**"I am very grateful to the general. But I wish to clarify that**

**I am a service member of the imperial medical corps, not a civilian volunteer."**

**"Forgive me, Countess. I had the mistaken idea that you worked with the Red Cross mission."**

**"No, Colonel. I am—I was—a first-year student in pediatric surgery at the medical university. I took my oath of service this past October as a training member of Doctor von Brenner's staff, and I was promoted to doctor's assistant in December as my work had proved satisfactory. I have taken a leave of absence from the university for the time being in order to devote myself fully to my work in the surgery. All this may be verified by the doctor, and by the faculty of the college of pediatrics at the university."**

**"Make a note of that, please, Lieutenant," Colonel Sosnkowski instructs the typist. "Continue, Countess."**

The boy was a peasant, a Ukrainian—as a matter of fact, Zarudce is predominantly a Ukrainian village, though there are of course a number of Polish households and some Jewish and German households too.

He was scuffed and dirty, this poor boy. Thin and knobby as a reed, with a bristle-brush head of white-blond hair cropped short and a runny nose. He was perhaps ten or eleven years old, perhaps younger. It's difficult to tell the ages of children in wartime because we must all grow up so quickly. He was old enough to cry, knees shaking, when they put the noose around his neck—old enough to understand what they were about to do.

I wondered, and still wonder, whether he understood why. They spoke no Ukrainian, and he spoke no German. But somebody in the village had told them he'd carried dispatches for the Russians during the occupation, so they were hanging him.

**This time, it's Captain Baran who interrupts.**

**"Colonel Sosnkowski, this can't possibly be relevant—"**

**"Be quiet, Baran," Colonel Sosnkowski orders. "Continue, Countess."**

I didn't try to stop them. I watched them do it.

We all watched them do it. There was a crowd of us—most of Zarudce, I should think, or most of those left after a year of Russian occupation and then the retreat. As you know, the Russians deported a great many of our people to camps in the east on suspicion either of collaboration with the Austrians or of revolutionary sentiment of our own. Most of us had personal reasons for wanting vengeance against the Russians and against anybody who had collaborated with them, and we all had seen summary executions before.

This was war. We all understood.

I don't think anyone observing me that day could've predicted that in six months' time I would be the one turning traitor, trying to atone for my failure to save one poor boy's life by saving another's. But—looking back now—I can see that was when the seeds of my betrayal were sown.

I went to find the boy's mother the next day. An old-fashioned sense of my duties as Countess Zamoyska, perhaps. It was what my mother would've done. She would've known the boy's family. I am ashamed to say I did not.

I went to the Greek Catholic church because I thought perhaps the priest would know. Most of the Ukrainians in Zarudce are Greek Catholics. Yes, the priest said, yes, he knew the family. He could end my search here.

The boy's father had died in the second month of the war. He had been an infantry conscript of General von Brudermann's army, and he died when the Russians took Lemberg in September of 1914. The boy's mother had died not quite three weeks before my inquiry. The Russians had come to burn the farm—they burned nearly every farm in Zarudce in June, during the retreat—and she had taken the family's Zaporozhian Cossack saber from its bracket on the wall, where I imagine it had hung for generations, and tried to stop them, and they had killed her. They had raped her first, judging by the state in which her body was apparently found.

The boy was an orphan at the Russians' hands, and we had hanged him as a collaborator.

And perhaps he *had* been a collaborator. Perhaps he *had* carried dispatches during the occupation. Perhaps he had done it for food or for money, or to save his mother's life, or to save his own life.

He didn't get a tribunal, that boy. He didn't have the opportunity to explain why he had done what he had done. As very few of our officers speak Ukrainian, it is unlikely—had he been given the opportunity after all—that anyone would've understood him anyway.

There are other reasons for my actions of four days ago, but the first reason, and the most important, is guilt.

# CHAPTER 3

Another reason, as I said, was the snowstorm.

We watched it building all that morning, moving down slowly from the northwestern hills—thick folds of soft, dove-gray clouds against a flat leaden sky.

I had been going back and forth by ambulance from the hospital to the central station across town, overseeing the collection and transfer of some badly wounded casualties who'd been sent down to us that morning from Sokal, ninety kilometers to the north. It is one of my duties as Doctor von Brenner's assistant to receive the wounded and to make note of which require surgery most urgently so that they may be prioritized accordingly when they reach the hospital. One of the medics who had accompanied the wounded on the train told me that theirs had been the last train out, as Sokal was already under heavy snow and they were worried about derailments.

At noon, when my shift was done, Doctor von Brenner suggested it might be best if I stayed in the city for the weekend. This was last Friday—the feast day of Saint Sylwester, New Year's Eve. As a matter of fact, the doctor offered to pay for a suite at the

Hotel George if I didn't want to stay at the hospital. We could tell it was going to be a bad storm, and Doctor von Brenner was concerned that if I went home to Zarudce I might end up getting snowed in. As we are understaffed at present, especially in the surgery, he hoped to avoid that.

He was absolutely right, as you know, but I turned him down. That was pride. I hadn't the money for a hotel—certainly not for a suite at the George, certainly not for the entire weekend if that was how things turned out—and I didn't want to be in his debt.

I've learned from experience that a man too easily gets mistaken ideas when a woman puts herself in his debt.

And it was perhaps a bit of vanity too: I hadn't brought an overnight bag. I had never needed one. I was on the overnight shift, twelve midnight to twelve noon, and I always went straight home when my shift was done. I didn't want to be stuck in the city for an entire weekend with nothing but the surgery-stained clothes on my back.

And of course I was reluctant to let the house stand empty for any length of time—

**"I beg your pardon, Countess." Colonel Sosnkowski again. "But to clarify, this is your typical schedule? Your daily schedule?"**

**"Yes, Colonel. Sunday nights through Friday mornings. I have Saturdays and Sunday mornings off. Doctor von Brenner can verify if you need."**

**"You mean to say you walk from Zarudce to Lemberg and back five days a week."**

**There's a distinct disadvantage to having one of my countrymen as my examiner, especially one as adept as Colonel**

**Sosnkowski. I doubt very much that General von Linsingen and his staff know how far Zarudce is from Lemberg. I doubt any of them could locate Zarudce on a map—just another one of countless insignificant little villages scattered through the hills around the city. But Colonel Sosnkowski, as Commandant Piłsudski's chief of intelligence, knows this region as well as I do, perhaps better. Nothing is hidden from him. His eyes and ears are everywhere around us, if one is to believe the rumors. I should've known this detail wouldn't be lost on him.**

**"On occasion," I admit, "Captain Baran has driven me in his motorcar. That's how I know from experience that a man gets mistaken ideas when a woman puts herself in his debt."**

**Captain Baran's face is flushed. "My mistake, Colonel Sosnkowski, was in thinking that the countess might wait more than three days to open her legs for a Muscovite peasant—"**

**"Enough," Colonel Sosnkowski snaps. "Make a note, please, Lieutenant—unauthorized use of matériel. That car is not for Captain Baran's personal leisure. Continue, Countess."**

I was reluctant to let the house stand empty, you understand, because I didn't want to lose it. A foolish thing to worry about, perhaps, especially during a snowstorm heavy enough to shut down every road and railway line within two hundred kilometers of Lemberg. I had no protection money to give the Russians last summer; they took everything they needed or wanted and burned the house and grounds in June, when they burned the rest of Zarudce, and though I was able to save part of the house itself, it is not an ideal place for wintering.

But still it was my house, my last tangible remembrance of everything and everyone I've lost.

It has become common practice nowadays for noble families

of our rank to maintain a residence in the city as well as the dwór, the traditional manor house, and to spend more time in the city than in the countryside. My father would have none of that. It was, to his mind, a moral imperative that the knightly class should be close to the land. He considered it shameful that so many of the szlachta nowadays have left the working of the land in the hands of managers and foremen. It was important to him that his children should know for themselves how to ride and hunt, plant and harvest, tend and cultivate and keep. He did keep a rowhouse in Lemberg, it's true, for my mother's use as her trips to the clinic grew more and more frequent. But Mieszko and I were brought up in Zarudce, in the shadow of the old-growth forest that stretches all across Galicia to the banks of the Vistula, nearly two hundred kilometers to the west.

They're buried there now, my mother and Mieszko. I buried them in our apple orchard on the hill above the garden. And though I never received my father's body back from the Russian prison camp at Sretensk, I've buried his medals there with his wife and his son. And I had this fear that one day I would come home to find somebody else had claimed the place in my absence, and I would have no recourse.

Of course—as you know—that is exactly what happened.

⁂

It was dark and already snowing when I got to the house. It was about four o'clock in the afternoon. It's more than a two-hour walk from Lemberg to Zarudce in the best of weather, and I had made a couple of stops on my way out of the city—at Altshuler's pharmacy for a bottle of cough syrup and then at the post office to pick up a parcel. We have neither a pharmacy nor a post office in Zarudce, and since I'm in the city so often, people ask me to run these sorts of errands for them.

The cough syrup was for the Kaplan boy; the parcel was for Pani Adamczyk. I decided I would make the deliveries in the morning because I was so tired and because the snow was by now starting to fall quite heavily.

A fateful decision, it turns out, because if I had made the deliveries that night, I am sure the Kaplans or Pani Adamczyk would have insisted I spend the night with them, and I would've been snowed in with them instead, and none of the rest would've followed. But I decided to wait until the morning.

My two unexpected visitors hadn't gotten a fire going yet—they had preceded me by a matter of minutes, I think—and either I was too tired to notice their footprints in the snow leading up to the kitchen stoop, or the snow had already covered the prints over again.

The door was unlocked already. I hadn't bothered to put new locks on any of the doors since June because all the windows in the great room, the fine Venetian glass windows my grandfather had put in to replace the old waxed canvas ones, were shattered anyway, and though I'd boarded them over as best I could before the weather turned, anyone could've pried the boards off and gotten into the house that way. It was quite easy to pry them off, as we found out later.

So I did not know the enemy were there until one of them had pulled me in from the doorway and flung me down to the floor in the corner between the stove and the woodbin. And in the pitch dark—he had kicked the door shut again—I did not know they were the enemy until one of them said to the other, "Wait, Adya." He said it in Russian: "Podozhdi, Adya."

**"Do you speak Russian, Countess?"**

**"Yes, Colonel. It was necessary during the occupation. And it has been helpful in my capacities at the hospital. Badly wounded prisoners come to us from the front before they're sent on to the camps, and very often we find that they require a translator. Most of them do not speak Polish even if they are themselves ethnic Poles, and almost none of them speak German. Doctor von Brenner—"**

**"Can verify if we need." A half smile twitches Colonel Sosnkowski's lips. "Make a note, please, Lieutenant. Continue, Countess."**

One of them struck a match, lighting all our faces briefly red-gold in the dark. He had the telltale dark marks on his coat where he had taken off his officer's shoulder boards and insignia. Their officers will do this sometimes in an attempt to avoid interrogation if they're taken prisoner; I expect ours do the same. I know to look for such marks because we are instructed to do so in the hospital when they bring in prisoners from the front.

The other, Adya, was the one who had pulled me in from the doorway and thrown me down. He stood between me and the door now. He had no officer's shoulder boards or insignia, but he had a pistol in his hand.

They were very obviously men on the run—quite apart from their Russian uniforms, I mean. They were hollow-cheeked and filthy, their bare fingers red with early frostbite, and even in the cold they stank. They both reeked of mud and sweat, but the one holding the match—the officer, the one who'd told Adya to wait—smelled of gangrene too. His dark eyes were shining bright with fever.

I've seen many gangrenous wounds in the hospital, and I did not need to see this one. I knew from the smell, sick-sweet and rotten, he would need amputation to live, and he would need it soon.

The match went out, and we were in darkness again.

I said in Russian, "There's a lamp on the shelf above the stove." I was still on my knees in the corner. I didn't dare get up while I couldn't see that pistol. I had dropped the bottle of cough syrup and Pani Adamczyk's parcel. The glass bottle had shattered on the stone floor; I could feel the syrup seeping slowly into the knees of my stockings. It had cost me ten crowns, that bottle—nearly a week's wages—though I wouldn't have told Pani Kaplan so.

The officer found the lamp on the shelf, moving slowly and with effort in the dark, and struck another match to light it. The soft glow of the flame fell around us, chasing the shadows away. The one called Adya said to me coldly, "What are you doing here?"

They had studied me in the match light too. They had seen my coat. I wore a dead Austrian boy's greatcoat. I have no other winter coat, and the wool is good quality and warm. I hadn't bothered to take off the shoulder boards or insignia. They could see it was an Austrian's coat.

"I live here," I told him. "This is my house."

"No one lives here."

I didn't blame him for thinking so. The house is partially burned and collapsed. The kitchen and great room are intact—they're the oldest part of the house, built centuries ago of white-washed clay an arm's length deep under a pitched gable roof of red ceramic tile, nearly impossible to burn—but the remainder of the house was done in timber and thatch much later, and that is what the Russians torched in June. I've sealed off the kitchen as best I can by stuffing rags and newspaper in the cracks around the doorways and closing up the window above the sink with piled stones and pieces of brick, and it keeps moderately warm when the stove is lit. But they could not have seen all these preparations in one quick glance by match light. From the outside, the house looks abandoned.

I could've proven myself to them very quickly by pulling up the loose stone before the cellar doorway and showing them my little stock of supplies in the hollow beneath: potatoes and pickled herring and bacon and plum jam and salt and a half-full bottle of krupnik. But I did not.

"This is my house," I repeated. "I work weeknights at the general hospital in Lemberg, but I live here."

"The hospital," Adya said.

"I work in the surgery. I've just come home."

"Lemberg is twelve kilometers from here."

"Yes."

They looked at me, then at each other. Adya still had the pistol in his hand. I could feel the wariness in him, taut and bristling.

The other one, the officer, was on his knees facing me, the stove between us, the spent match in his fingers. He was the younger of the two—a boy, really; his face was smooth. He was sixteen, perhaps, or seventeen, slender and pale and dark-eyed. Adya was a few years older, nineteen or twenty. There was a scattering of fair, sandy stubble on his jaw and a lean hardness to his face.

They were an odd pair. The boy was an officer, but Adya was quite clearly the one with authority here, and the boy didn't seem to mind.

Adya said to me coolly, "If you live here, then there must be something to eat here."

I should've counted myself lucky, of course, that they only wanted food. I should've shown them what was under the loose stone then; it was foolish of me not to. I had dealt with desperate, armed men more than once before, and I knew very well that it was best to preempt them by offering things that could be replaced. Better to part voluntarily with potatoes and krupnik before they set their minds on what I wasn't offering.

But in that moment, tired as I was, I admit I did not care.

You may think whatever you wish of me. My reputation certainly isn't above reproach at this point.

When they finished with me, they would leave, in search of what could be had elsewhere, or they would shoot me, and it would not matter one way or another. But I did not want them to take the food. I had worked hard for that food.

"I have nothing," I told them. "There was nothing left at the butcher's. I couldn't go until after my shift, and there was nothing."

Adya motioned with the pistol to Pani Adamczyk's parcel. "What is that?"

"It isn't mine. I'm bringing it to a friend in the village."

"Open it."

"Adya . . ." the boy said.

"It isn't mine," I said.

"Open it," Adya insisted.

He leveled the pistol at my head, and I opened the parcel. If I lived, I would apologize to Pani Adamczyk. I would offer to pay her for the trouble.

The parcel was a cardboard box wrapped in brown paper and tied up with twine, postmarked in Kowel with a stamp bearing the imperial Habsburg eagle. The contents were light and loose, rattling about as I undid the twine. It took me a little while as my fingers were so cold, and it didn't help to have that pistol pointed at me the whole time.

I sat on my knees and turned the cardboard box out onto the lap of my coat. There was a cheap brass pocket watch and a rosary and a Saint Christopher on a chain, all knotted up together; a bronze Medal for Bravery, with its cameo of the emperor, on a fold of scarlet-and-white ribbon; and a little leather-bound prayer book with gilt-edged pages and the inscription *To Leonek 1915.*

They were a dead boy's things. This wouldn't have been the first time I'd delivered such a parcel to a mother in Zarudce. They are the lucky ones, the mothers and wives who receive parcels, because that means at least that their loved ones have been found and identified and given a burial.

For a moment, we were all three silent, looking. Then, in a flash, Adya reached down, pulled me up by an elbow—as haggard as he looked, he was surprisingly strong—and dragged me over to the kitchen table, scattering Leo Adamczyk's things all across the floor.

But he did not do what I thought he meant to do.

He sat me down in one of the chairs and tied my wrists to the chair back with the length of twine from the parcel. He did it very cleverly, one wrist to each side, so I couldn't reach one hand to the other and try to loosen the knots that way.

The knots were not unduly tight; I could move my hands a little. But I was stuck fast in that chair.

"They patrol here," I told him. "A cavalry troop of the Polish Legions patrols these grounds every night. Their officer is my fiancé"—I am not proud of this part—"and he always stops in to see that I'm safe."

“For your sake,” Adya said into my ear—he was behind me, tugging at the knots to test them—“I hope you’re lying. You’ll be the first to die.”

Across the room, the young officer picked up Leo Adamczyk’s things one by one and returned them very carefully to the box.

# CHAPTER 4

You may note that none of this so far had been my choice. None of this had been willing collaboration. I had not offered them my food or indeed anything of mine. I had not offered them medical assistance, though the boy needed it badly. I had done my best, alone and unarmed as I was, to frighten them into leaving by telling them that the Legions patrolled the manor grounds.

I suppose I could've refused to open that parcel or made some other provocation that would've compelled them to shoot me. Perhaps that would've been the most honorable course.

But if following an order under the threat of a gun makes me a collaborator, then any of our soldiers who allow themselves to be taken prisoner are collaborators. As Commandant Piłsudski has himself survived the ordeal of Russian captivity—

**An angry stirring from Captain Baran interrupts me. "Colonel Sosnkowski—"**

**"Continue, Countess," Colonel Sosnkowski says, ignoring him.**

I presume it is not the commandant's opinion that following a Russian order for survival's sake makes one a collaborator.

If the story ended here—if the snowstorm had subsided just then and my unwanted visitors had left; if the Legions had in fact patrolled the manor grounds; if Captain Baran and his troop had come upon us at this moment rather than three days later—I think you would all agree, with the possible exception of Captain Baran, that I could hardly be accused of disrupting the war effort.

But of course the story does not end here.

They had come, as best as I could tell, from the temporary holding camp here in Lemberg. I don't know how else Adya could've known that Lemberg was a twelve-kilometer walk. They had no map, no compass, no supplies I could see besides that pistol, which was a Mauser, German made, and which I presumed they had taken from a guard when they made their escape from the camp. But if they had used the Lemberg road, they of course would've seen the kilometer marker when they came into Zarudce. I doubt men in their condition could've made it to Zarudce from one of the prison camps farther west.

It became clear to me that they had stopped not only because of the approaching storm but because the boy, whom Adya called Vitya, was too sick to walk much farther. He sat hunched and shivering by the stove, coat pulled tightly about himself, cap tugged low over his ears, while Adya moved about carefully by lamplight, making a search of the kitchen and the cellar.

He had come to believe me that this was my house, or at least that I was living here. He found my bit of lard soap and my comb and the night pot in the corner, and he found the empty feed sacks I was using for blankets and turned them inside out to see if there were any old kernels caught in the seams; then he brought them over to Vitya. But he would not believe me when I told him there was no food.

He made a practiced and thorough search, such as only one who is well acquainted with hunger could make. He opened each of my kitchen cupboards one after another, kneeling and reaching in to run his hand along the sides and backs. He stood on a chair to search the top of the tall wooden hutch that once held my grandmother Helena's bone china; he pulled out each drawer and turned it over in his hands. He took the cellar steps one by one, pausing to feel beneath each step. He did not spend very long in the cellar. The soil has been frozen solid since the end of November. Anything buried down there will remain buried until the spring thaw.

He found several things I wished he had not found, things that made me feel more vulnerable than being tied to that chair.

He found Grandmother Helena's tablecloth, the fine silk one she made from her wedding dress, wrapped in butcher paper behind the sink. Even the Russians in June hadn't found it, but he did.

He found the sheet music for Chopin's waltz in C-sharp minor that I'd slipped between the underside of the drawer and the slats in the hutch.

He found the letters from Emi, addressed to me in the lovely formal Polish that I can only imagine Emi taught himself out of old poetry books—*Renia, ukochana moja . . .*

Adya spent a moment looking at the sheet music; he didn't touch the letters except to move them. He couldn't read Polish, I supposed, if he could read at all.

But he did not find the loose stone before the cellar doorway. I'm always careful to smooth sand along the edges so it isn't obvious that the stone has been recently moved and replaced. It's difficult to spot even by daylight. It is impossible by lamplight unless one knows exactly where to look.

He gave up finally, slamming a last cupboard door shut in one swift outburst of frustration. He did not look at me or speak to me. He snapped something I didn't catch to Vitya and went outside. The door blew wide in a sudden gust of wind when he opened it. Snow scurried across the kitchen floor like fine white flour dusting a pastry board. He pulled the door shut again behind him with some effort and vanished out into the dark.

When he came back, quite some time later, he was carrying an armful of young birch boughs. There are white birches in a copse along the Zarudce road; he must've noted them earlier. Snow was furred thickly on his cap and on the shoulders of his coat. He had his scarf tied about his mouth and nose, leaving only the space around his eyes uncovered beneath the brim of his cap, but his hands were still bare, red as beets. I could tell that frostbite on his fingers would become serious if he wasn't more careful with his hands.

This time, I heard what he said to the boy: "I can't see ni khuya." It's nearly the same in Russian and Polish—*ni khuya, ni chuja. I can't see a fucking thing.*

I admit I was surprised he came back.

It hadn't crossed the boy's mind, I don't think, but it had crossed mine. By this time, I'd had the chance to study both of them more closely in the lamplight, and I had started piecing together a story. Adya was a commoner, an enlisted man or perhaps a conscript. Vitya was highborn; I could tell by his hands. Even frostbitten, the skin was smooth and uncallused. He had long, slim fingers, musician's fingers, that had almost certainly never touched a plow or a sickle.

He'd most likely been given his commission; he was too young to have earned it. He was some imperial official's son, promoted on account of his father's title and money. He had done something foolhardy and gotten himself wounded—he was favoring his left foot; he had, most likely, shot himself so as to avoid being sent up the line.

I have seen it happen. I do not judge men who self-inflict wounds. It is not my place to judge from one hundred and fifty kilometers behind the front.

In any case, the boy had ended up a prisoner, and Adya, out of duty or pity, had gotten him out of the hell of the holding camp, but now the boy could walk no farther, and Adya had no more reason to stay.

He had brought him this far, to someplace relatively warm and dry. He had done as much as anybody could ask, and much more than some might expect. I imagine there is as little love lost between the Russian peasantry and nobility as there is between our own classes.

**Colonel Sosnkowski says, "Do you consider yourself to be a socialist, Countess?"**

**"My brother was a member of the Party, Colonel. I am not, if that's what you mean."**

**"But one could infer that you are sympathetic to the ideology. You are speaking of class conflict."**

**He is not offended or scandalized. He's a socialist himself, as is Commandant Piłsudski. But he is, perhaps, surprised.**

**I don't blame him. My father's conservatism was well known. He was not old-fashioned in all of his sensibilities, my**

**father—for instance, he wouldn't have forbidden his daughter to attend medical school, had he lived long enough to see me make that choice. And he took very seriously the clinical treatment of my mother's melancholia, when another man of his age and social set might've dismissed it as womanly nonsense. But he remained unconvinced of the usefulness of socialism in the struggle for Polish independence. He considered the class struggle to be a distraction.**

**It was a point of contention between him and Mieszko, who came back three years ago from Commandant Piłsudski's paramilitary training school in Kraków with a membership in the Polish Socialist Party and a head full of progressive ideas. They differed not in objectives—they were both ardent Polish patriots to the end—but in methods and means.**

**"I haven't sat down and formulated every one of my political positions, Colonel. But when an Austrian freiherr and a Ukrainian conscript are brought into the surgery, I know who will be the first to receive treatment. And I can assure you that they do too."**

Adya had taken the pistol when he left the house. I had not thought he would be back. And yet here he was, pulling his scarf from his face and kneeling beside Vitya to warm his hands at the stove.

Perhaps he had changed his mind. Perhaps the snow was falling too heavily now, and he didn't know the lay of the land well enough to risk it, at least not in the dark. The forest lay to the west of us, but to the east—toward the Russian lines, presumably the direction he would be trying to go—there was nothing but vast open farmland, stripped bare in the Russians' retreat. In a bad snow, it's dangerous to be caught in the open. He was desperate, but he was no fool.

In any case, my threat was of course empty to him now. If he could hardly see to find his way two hundred meters to the birches, the Legions would not be sending out a patrol tonight.

When his hands were warm, Adya set to work on the birch boughs. He sat cross-legged beside Vitya and took a pocketknife from somewhere inside his coat—I hadn't known he had that knife, and it made me wonder what else I'd missed.

He split the fleshy inner bark from the hardwood, turning each bough smoothly in his hand and cutting away the bark in long strips. He discarded the hardwood, tossing it onto the woodpile piece by piece; then he peeled the paper-thin outer bark from the inner bark and scooped the bare inner bark by handfuls into my cooking pot. Then he filled the pot to the brim with clean snow and set it on the stove to boil.

It shamed me, sitting there in my chair and watching him work. From the swiftness and skillfulness of his movements, it was clear he'd done this before.

I've done without in this war; I have gone hungry. I have eaten with my fingers and not cared. I do not remember the last time I ate meat that was not cured or dried or from a tin. But—even last summer, when the Russians took everything they could put their hands on and cut down my mother's apple trees and burned our cornfield—I have never been hungry enough to boil tree bark for food.

*People like us will never be the ones bearing the brunt of war,* Mieszko wrote to me once in those first few weeks before Lemberg fell. He'd lost the bulk of his unit—conscripts, most of them, forced to be there—under heavy artillery fire at the Gniła Lipa before the order to retreat finally came down from the high command, and his frustration had boiled over.

And he was right. Even in deprivation, I have a roof over my head each night and a steady income of fifty crowns per month, which is more than most people in Zarudce can say—certainly more than any frontline soldier can say, on either side. I don't let myself forget that.

Still I did not tell them what was under the loose stone.

When the birch bark was soft, they ate it like stewed meat, chewing small bites slowly and carefully, making it last. They took turns drinking the boiled birch snow from the pot, like tea. In all honesty, the stuff didn't look bad or smell bad. The flesh of the bark was a pale reddish gold, quite lovely, and the steam from the pot smelled sweet and pungent and earthy, like old leaves and Christmas greenery.

Vitya caught me watching. He swallowed his mouthful and leaned over almost shyly to say something into Adya's ear, and Adya said, without looking up from the pot, "No."

"Pozhaluysta, Adya," the boy said—*please.*

"I'm not going to sit there spoon-feeding her."

For the first time, I began to feel a little twist of panic in the pit of my stomach—not that they wouldn't feed me but that they wouldn't untie me. I wouldn't have eaten or drunk anything just then even if they'd offered—for shame or for pride, I'm not sure. But I was afraid to be tied to that chair much longer. Sooner or later, I would have to relieve myself, and I did not want to do it in front of them, and I did not want to be tied there sitting in it.

And in truth it all seemed unnecessary. There were two of them, and they had a pistol and a knife. I could hardly have taken both of them by surprise. And Adya had been outside; he'd said himself that you couldn't see *ni khuya* in the snow. Where was I to go if I were to get away?

But I suppose he had to assume that I knew the ground better than he—that I could make it to the village and back with reinforcements even in such a storm.

When they had finished their meal of birch bark, Adya filled the empty pot with more snow and set it to boil again. He crouched at Vitya's feet and took off the boy's boots, tugging them by the heels and setting them aside on the hearth. He unwrapped the boy's thin, dirty foot cloths and put them in the pot.

"You don't have to," Vitya said. "It's all right."

"I'm going to wash these."

"I think it's getting better. It doesn't hurt as much."

"I know," Adya said.

The rotten stench spread thick and heavy on the close air. The boy's left foot was black to the ankle with gas gangrene. Adya didn't seem to notice. He took one of the boiled foot cloths and tore it in two. He held the boy's foot in his hand and washed it with the torn cloth, dipping the cloth back into the pot now and again as he worked, his hands steady and careful and surprisingly gentle.

"That's got to mean it's getting better, doesn't it?" Vitya asked. "If it doesn't hurt as much?"

"Yes," Adya said.

"If it were infected, it would hurt."

"Yes."

I sat there in my chair, listening. I did not tell them they were wrong.

# CHAPTER 5

I wonder sometimes at God's sense of humor. I suppose that's not very reverent of me. But it seems clear that He does have one. If we can laugh, then surely God must laugh, as we are bearers of His image, and I do occasionally feel that He must be laughing at *me*.

For instance, these past four days, as I've waited for this tribunal and then the firing squad, have been more restful and leisurely than any I can remember for some time—certainly since the war began.

My cell is a converted servant's bedroom, perhaps the cook's, just down the stairs from the kitchen, quite comfortably appointed. There is no bell ringing at all hours to summon me to the surgery. No cold, congealed semolina kasza eaten hurriedly on my feet in the anteroom between operations. I have three hot meals prepared for me each day. I do not have to scrounge the food or cook it or wash up afterward. My clothes are laundered for me and returned neatly folded and pressed. I can have books from Count Potocki's library brought to me upon request.

I'm allowed outside for a twenty-minute constitutional on

the estate grounds each afternoon, and there is no one to interrupt me or intrude upon me. Even my guards are kind enough to hang back at some distance and allow me my privacy. I don't think anyone really believes I am going to try to make a break for it, considering my broken rib.

I've had more time to myself while I wait to die—more time to indulge in my own thoughts—than I think I ever had as a free woman.

Even before the war, when my life could hardly have been considered difficult or my schedule taxing, my time was not my own. My days were taken up with the various activities and engagements requisite for the modern European noblewoman: my mornings with correspondence and the business of the household, my afternoons with luncheons and teas and garden parties, my evenings with dinners and dances and symphonies and operas and plays.

How trivial it all seems now. How very clearly we see our lives for what they are when we are about to die.

So I've had a good deal of time these past four days, as I've sat alone in my cell and waited for Commandant Piłsudski to arrive from the front so that this tribunal might be convoked, to think back and consider which was the exact moment I turned traitor—I mean the moment I made my conscious choice.

If you believe, as I've been brought up to believe, in the sovereign will of God and in the perfection of His providence, that not one thread of the divine tapestry is out of place, perhaps my entire life was building inevitably to that moment. And not only my life but, in a sense, every life ever lived, every war ever fought—the entire course of history, leading inexorably to my house that night in Zarudce. Perhaps there was never any other possible ending to this story.

It is a beautiful and terrifying thought.

But the moment itself, as near as I can determine, came in the freezing pitch dark of my cellar, where I had gone to relieve myself.

Vitya was fast asleep, curled up on the hearth near the stove with his coat and the empty feed sacks pulled tightly about him. He had fallen asleep almost at once when Adya finished tending his foot. I recognized that bone-deep exhaustion. His body was worn out from fighting itself.

Adya sat beside him against the wall, protective as a watchdog. He had put out the lamp—to conserve the oil, I supposed—and the only light was the soft red glow coming through the grille of the stove.

We were sitting in silence in that almost-dark, he and I, listening to the howl and rush of the wind and the creaking of tree limbs up in the wood. He sat very still and quiet, his head and shoulders braced against the wall, his arms at his sides. He had the pistol still in his hand; the light from the stove picked out the cold, gleaming blued metal of the barrel. His face was entirely obscured in the shadow of the stove, but I knew he was not asleep. I've learned in the hospital to tell by the pattern of the breaths.

I said to him finally—I was beyond any thought of pride or dignity at this point, and there was no reason not to be blunt—"I need to use the pot."

For a moment, I thought perhaps I was wrong and he was asleep after all, because he didn't move or speak or indeed give any indication that he had heard. But then, moving very slowly, as if he had to gather himself together first, he pushed up from the wall and came over to me. He knelt at my back and cut the twine from my wrists with his pocketknife.

He cut the twine; he did not untie it. It was, as I thought, his first slip in judgment. He would not be able to use it to tie me up again.

"Cellar," he said—one word in command.

I was caught off guard. That he would let me up so easily after all, that he had the decency to allow me the privacy of the cellar, that he would make such a careless mistake. Perhaps that's why I said to him, pausing at the cellar door with the night pot in my hands, "It's gangrenous. That wound."

We were facing each other across the table in the dark—I was not going to press my luck or his patience by asking him for the lamp—and I heard the soft hiss of his breath. "Yes."

"He needs it off. The entire foot. If he's going to live, he needs it off."

I was not offering my help, you will note. I was simply observing the facts.

And Adya said to me, low and calm across the table in the dark, very careful not to raise his voice and wake the boy, "I've spent the past three days in that fucking cattle pen of a holding camp in Lemberg, begging them to take him to the hospital, begging them to let a surgeon see him, begging them for the supplies to do it myself, and now you're going to tell me what he needs?"

Of course you all know as well as I that our Lemberg hospitals are overcrowded and understaffed. And that our own soldiers are given priority over prisoners when beds become available, as I am sure the enemy give priority to their own wounded in their own hospitals. And that immediately life-threatening wounds are given priority over wounds such as the boy's, particularly those that are self-inflicted or suspected to be so. A bullet to the ankle would not have gotten that boy a bed in any hospital within two hundred kilometers of the front, and might very easily have gotten him a firing squad.

That the wound had gone to gangrene was either bad luck—an inexperienced medic operating quickly with unsterilized instruments, perhaps—or divine retribution, depending on one's point of view. In any case, it was not deliberate mistreatment.

But of course there's no use trying to explain to a line soldier that his comrade is going to die from what should've been an easily treatable wound for no other reason than logistics.

It occurred to me, once I had felt my way carefully in the dark down the cellar steps, that Adya had made another slip in judgment. One can, of course, access the outside from that cellar. There's a second flight of steps and a pair of flat exterior doors opening outward to the yard. He could not have missed them when he searched the cellar. He had forgotten, I supposed, or he had assumed the doors were chained and padlocked shut from the outside, which they had been until June but were no longer.

Then it occurred to me that he did not care.

He had not forgotten about the cellar doors. He simply did not care whether I made it away to the village to raise an alarm or to bring a troop of the Legions. He had seen the progression of the gangrene, and he knew the boy was going to die, and nothing else mattered to him anymore.

That was the moment, Colonel Sosnkowski—Commandant Piłsudski—officers.

I was free to go. They would not have stopped me. They had taken neither my coat nor my boots from me. The storm was bad but not yet impassable as it would become. And I do know the ground quite well. I could've made the kilometer across the open fields to the Kaplans' farm or the two kilometers down the road to the village proper.

I could have, but I did not.

Having finished my business, I went up the steps and opened the exterior doors—with effort, because it had been snowing for some time now and a layer of soft, powdery snow nearly half a meter deep had drifted upon the surface of the doors. I spent a moment standing there at the top of the steps and looking out into the yard.

Under the circumstances, it was remarkable how peaceful everything seemed. How clean the air was, how pure and bright the fresh-fallen snow, how lovely the forest looked with the snow frosting the dark pine boughs like confectioner's sugar. The wind had stopped just then, and everything was very still and silent as though the entire world were waiting, breath drawn, to see what I would do—as though this were the most important choice I would ever make. Looking back now, it seems clear that it was.

This is the honest truth of it: I did not want to let that boy die.

I've wondered quite a lot about what would've happened if I had tried to stop the hanging of that Ukrainian boy in July—if I could've stopped them, if they would've deferred to me as Countess Zamoyska.

Of course one thing that this war has made very plain is how little a title really means when all our social niceties have been stripped away. And in any case, they were Austrians, and I am a Pole; they were armed men, and I am a woman.

But perhaps the mere fact that *someone* was stepping up to stop them would've been enough. Perhaps there were others in that crowd who might've stepped up too, if only I had been the first. Perhaps not—who knows? Perhaps I would've accomplished nothing. Perhaps they would've hanged the boy just the same. Perhaps they would've hanged me then too, as they hanged Count Potocki.

I don't know because I didn't try.

I shut the doors and climbed back up the steps to the kitchen.

"I can do it," I said to Adya.

He was crouched in front of the stove. He had the grille open. He was shifting the old logs with the point of a birch stick—I have no poker—and stirring up the embers in preparation to lay more wood on. I'm not sure he had heard my footsteps. He tensed there on his heels and looked up at me, his face red-gold in the flickering glow of the embers.

"The amputation," I said. "I can do it."

For a moment, he was very still, looking at me. Then he turned his face back to the fire. He laid three more logs on, one at a time, arranging them carefully with the birch stick and his bare hand.

He said finally, "With what?"

"There's a bow saw in the woodshed."

It fell to me to keep our woodshed full during the occupation. These days the Kaplan boy, Berek, comes by once a week to chop wood for me in exchange for a copy of the Lemberg newspaper, but Pani Kaplan wouldn't let him out of her sight during the occupation, lest the Russians conscript him. And of course Mieszko couldn't do it on account of his wounds.

That shamed him, I know. Not because I was a woman doing what he regarded as a man's work—he was never so small-minded. He was, I think, far prouder and more excited when I applied to medical school than I was myself. He took to calling me "Doctor Zamoyska," and only partly because he knew it irritated me. But he was never the sort to sit idly by when there was work to be done.

In any case, I'm quite accustomed to using that saw, and I have the calluses to prove it. It's the sort of thing I don't think twice about now—though it is odd to step back and consider that two years ago, nearly to the day, I was on Emi's arm, being presented to the emperor in the grand ballroom at the Hofburg in Vienna.

Who in that ballroom in January of 1914 could've pictured me calmly suggesting the use of the bow saw in my woodshed to remove a gangrenous limb?

"You think," Adya said, his fury slow and calm and precise, "you think I'm going to let you work on him with a fucking bow saw?"

"You can do it yourself if you don't trust me. But it needs to be done, and that's what I've got."

"A fucking bow saw."

I thought that was the end of it. I had offered; he had refused. I would have to live with the guilt of knowing I had offered aid to the enemy—I was fully conscious even then of what I had done, and of the ramifications—but I would not have to live with the guilt of knowing I might've saved that boy's life and did not try.

Then his voice came over to me again through the almost-dark. "Have you done it before?"

"Yes."

He shut the grille. I heard his long, low breath. "All right."

It was, by this time, around midnight, to judge roughly by the rate at which he had stoked the fire since the stove was lit. Circumstances had been leading to this moment for six months, or for eighteen years, or for all of eternity. But in the strictest sense of things, which is what I suppose concerns this tribunal, it had taken me less than eight hours to turn traitor.

# CHAPTER 6

You know the rest, I think.

You've seen the coroner's report—it was deemed necessary to have a coroner's report filed with the Red Cross, given young Captain Witkowski's importance. He was of a prominent Russian-Polish family; his great-grandfather was the Russian-installed president of Warsaw during the January Uprising fifty years ago—a man much hated by his own people, as you know, but esteemed by the Russians for his usefulness. And the boy himself was aide-de-camp to General Brusilov, commander of the Russian Eighth Army, though of course I was unaware of all this at the time.

At any rate, you know Captain Witkowski was dead by the next day.

In all honesty, I did not expect him to last so long. The gangrene was quite advanced, and his immune system was already severely compromised by malnutrition, quite apart from the bacterial infection.

And of course amputation is a risky business in the best of circumstances. Even in modern hospitals with modern equipment, five percent of patients will die after amputation, on average—one in twenty. It does not seem like so many, perhaps, until one considers how many hundreds of wounded arrive at the hospital each week. There are many days when we perform amputations on more than twenty patients.

There is, I believe, little else I can tell you that you do not already know from Captain Baran's testimony. No one reading Gibbon can claim to be surprised that Rome has fallen.

**"But one may still be surprised at how and why," Colonel Sosnkowski observes.**

**"I've offered an explanation, Colonel."**

**"You've explained why you felt an obligation to assist Captain Witkowski."**

**"Yes. With respect, I believe that was the question."**

**"Captain Witkowski was dead the morning of January first, Countess, by your own testimony and corroborated by the coroner's report. But you were arrested on the morning of the third for—speaking bluntly, with your pardon—offering Captain Baran sexual favors in exchange for Lieutenant Kijek's release, and you have not denied the charge."**

**"In exchange for Lieutenant Kijek's life, Colonel."**

**"I beg your pardon?"**

**"I wish to clarify that I did not ask Captain Baran for the lieutenant's release. I asked him to spare the lieutenant's life, in accordance with the protocols regarding the treatment of prisoners of war. I had reason to believe—from my own acquaintance with Captain Baran and my judgment of his character—I had reason to believe that Lieutenant Kijek's life would've been in danger had he been left alone in Captain Baran's custody."**

"She was sleeping with him," Captain Baran bursts out. "She was sleeping with the Muscovite, and it's my character in question here?"

"Regardless"—Colonel Sosnkowski's voice is cold and tight—"it would be fair to say, Countess, that Captain Witkowski's life was no longer your primary concern by the morning of the third."

In his seat under guard at the back of the room, Lieutenant Kijek has leaned forward as if straining to hear. He doesn't speak German, but he has heard his name. He must know the turn the discussion has taken.

"No, Colonel. You are right. It was not."

"Then, if you please, Countess—continue."

# CHAPTER 7

It is a peculiar flaw of human nature—of our fallen nature—that when we have made one moral concession, we find it easier to make another.

Father Urban, our priest in Zarudce, calls this the searing of the conscience. When we have justified one failing in one moment of weakness, it becomes easier and easier to justify others, until we've become entirely desensitized to wrongdoing.

**Colonel Sosnkowski says with curiosity, "Do you consider your actions to have been a moral failing, Countess?"**

**"I have said I have no argument against the charges. I believe most people consider prostitution to be a moral failing."**

**"That wasn't my question. You would agree with me, I presume, that legality is not always the same as morality, and that illegality is not always the same as immorality. In your own opinion, Countess—this court and the charges aside—do you believe your actions constituted a moral failing?"**

**"You mean a sin."**

**"For the purposes of the question—yes, let's consider them synonymous."**

**I weigh my answer carefully. "I took an oath of unconditional loyalty to the empire, and I broke it. To my mind, yes, that is a sin. I was brought up to believe in the sacredness of giving one's word. That is why I have no argument against the charges. I am fully prepared to accept the consequences of my actions. It was, I think, less of a sin to break my oath than it would've been to let both Captain Witkowski and Lieutenant Kijek die, but I recognize that the degrees of sin are not for this tribunal to decide."**

**"No—I don't feel qualified to settle that debate," Colonel Sosnkowski says. "It will have to be taken up by a higher court. My fault for asking the question. Please continue, Countess."**

What I mean to say is that I no longer felt the need to conceal the loose stone before the cellar door from Adya. I knelt to pull it up carefully. We were still going only by the light of the stove as we made our preparations; we had not yet woken Vitya. I gave Adya the bottle of krupnik to give to the boy.

"Don't let him drink all of it. I haven't got anything else to use as an antiseptic."

Adya had knelt beside me on the cold flagstone floor, near enough that our knees were touching, his left against my right. Near enough that I could feel the brush of his coat sleeve against mine, and the gust of his breath on my cheek, and his warmth; he was running a slight fever too. I could hear his soft inhalation when he caught sight of what was under the stone.

He spent a moment leaning down, investigating with his frostbitten fingers, feeling through each of the crinkled butcher-paper packages in turn: bacon, and dried brown river trout, and—he swore quietly in astonishment when he came upon this—a jar of salt-brined herring pickled in vinegar, a luxury indeed. Herring must of course be brought down from Danzig or one of the other Baltic ports, or brought up from Odessa or elsewhere on the Black Sea, and it has been quite difficult to get since the war started. That jar was given to me as a Christmas gift out of one of his Red Cross parcels by an officer of the Polish Legions whom I treated in hospital—a precious reminder of our Christmas Eve Wigilia feasts in years past, when we would've eaten it with mushroom soup and pierogi and cabbage rolls and gingerbread once the first star had been sighted in the night sky.

Of course I—with the frugality one learns in wartime—had not eaten any of that herring for Wigilia but had laid it up until I should really have need of it.

Adya counted the potatoes one by one. He snatched up the little pot of plum jam and held it in his hand for a moment as though to make sure it was not just some trick of the light. This close, I could feel the hunger alive in him; I could feel him shivering with it. There was light enough from the stove that I could see the way his hands shook.

But he took nothing. If he was angry that I'd lied to him earlier—that I had sat there holding my tongue and watching him boil birch bark to eat—he didn't show it. He put the pot of jam back down very slowly and sat back on his heels, letting out his breath again in a soft little laugh.

I took the jar of pickled herring and opened it on my lap and put a piece of fish in his hand.

I've tended many cases of malnutrition in the hospital. Most of the prisoners who come to us from the front are afflicted with it to one extent or another, even the officers. I know the danger in allowing a starving man to eat too much too quickly. If I hadn't seen him eat that bark and keep it down, I wouldn't have offered him the fish—at least, I wouldn't have offered it to him like that; I would've made him wait until I had boiled it in a broth.

But at any rate he didn't cram it into his mouth all at once, as I expected. He held it carefully and started over to where Vitya was lying still asleep before the stove.

I caught his coat sleeve. "No—for you."

He looked at me blankly. "Then give him some."

"After."

"Now."

"It will slow the effect of the alcohol if he eats now. But you need to be able to hold him down. You need to be stronger than he is, do you understand?"

He was silent for a moment. Then he nodded once, and I let go of his sleeve.

He stood over the table and ate two pieces of pickled fish in measured mouthfuls, as he had eaten the birch bark—clearly he, too, was well aware of the danger in eating too quickly on an empty stomach.

I set to work prying away the bits of brick and gravel with which I'd filled in the broken window above the sink. I carved out a little crevice and put the lamp there so that its light could be seen from the woodshed.

The snow was falling fiercely now, driven along by the wind, and I didn't want to take any chances. I didn't want to lose sight of the house and stray blindly in the wrong direction. East of the house, as I've said, there is nothing but open farmland until Kulików, seven kilometers away. It does not take very long to die if one is caught in the open in such a snow.

There was only one match left in my matchbox. Pani Kaplan had promised me another box as part of my payment for the cough syrup that was spilled below the woodbin now. I hadn't considered the need urgent because I hadn't supposed that I would use more than one match before the morning, when I should've taken the syrup to her. But Vitya had used two.

I dipped a birch twig in lamp oil, caught the end afire in the stove, and used that to light the lamp. I said to Adya, "We can't let the stove go out. I haven't got any other way to relight it. I haven't got a flint."

"We'll take shifts," he said, "you and I. One of us will always be awake."

I did not, as Captain Baran has suggested, open my legs for Lieutenant Kijek that night, or any of the days and nights that followed. Nor did he ever expect that I would. But I will credit the captain with being right about one thing. How easy it was, how little time it took, for us to stop thinking of each other as enemies.

# CHAPTER 8

I suppose before I go any further I should tell you something more of the house and grounds so you all may have an accurate picture, since the lay of the land came to play such a part in the events that unfolded.

The house, what remains of it, sits facing eastward on the shoulder of a long, bare hill. Our cornfield lay at the very foot of the hill in the rich bottomlands along the river; above it was the fenced grazing land for our milk cattle and my father's horses. Nearer the house were the various small outbuildings: beehouses, henhouse, pigsty, woodshed, summer kitchen, brewery, smokery. There was a kitchen garden in the yard behind the house where we grew cucumbers and cabbage, beets and turnips. My mother's apple orchard was on the slope of the hill above the garden.

And then the forest, vast and dark and ancient, where we gathered chestnuts and blackberries, acorns and wild onions, and where my father and Mieszko and our woodsmen went out to hunt deer and elk and boar.

West of the house, going toward the Młynówka River, the

wood is mostly oak and pine, but southward, in the direction of Lemberg, there's a belt of towering old mountain larches. They grow quite close along the southern side of the house, those larches, and some of them must be thirty meters tall—quite close enough and tall enough to do serious damage to the roof of the house should they fall.

I suppose it was inevitable that one of them would fall eventually, as the wind has always been quite fierce over the bare shoulder of that hill, and we've had trouble with downed tree limbs before. In fact my father had those trees cut back once, because they'd started to overhang the grazing land and he was concerned about the risk they posed to the animals. Of my parents, I do think my father was the more softhearted one.

But of course we neglect mundane things like that in wartime. I hadn't given a thought in years to those larch trees and the peculiar danger they posed. There had been so many other, more pressing dangers to worry about, especially as I have no stock to let out to graze anymore. Our milk cow was the last, and the Russians took her in June.

I know I am to be sentenced for "actions deemed disruptive to the war effort," and everything else is ultimately rather peripheral. But I must say that there is something ironic in surviving all the dangers and hardships and deprivations of wartime only to come to ruin because I didn't cut those larches back.

It's a straight line of about twenty meters across the yard from the kitchen stoop to the woodshed, which sits just under the eaves of the forest. To be strictly technical, of course, my woodshed burned in June along with the stock barn and the grain barn and the henhouse and all the other wooden outbuildings. The outbuilding that I use now as a woodshed is what used to be the smokery. It's built of whitewashed clay, like the kitchen and the great room, and too much trouble to burn.

I made that first crossing without much difficulty. I could see the light in the kitchen window over my shoulder all the way across the yard. The wind was bad, but it was gusting mainly east to west—at my back as I went toward the woodshed, not in my face—and the house served as something of a windbreak.

In the woodshed, the first thing I did was take down a goodly length of hauling rope from the wall and knot it securely to the eye of the door latch. I would trail the rope back across the yard and knot it again at the kitchen stoop, and we would have a lifeline running between the kitchen and the woodshed much as they have on decks of ships when waves are breaking over the railing. Next I gathered up an armful of split logs, as many as I could carry, and took down the bow saw.

It was then I noticed that the light in the kitchen window had gone out.

My first thought—as I stood there in the woodshed doorway with the rope in one numb hand and the saw in the other, my arms and shoulders straining under the weight of the logs—was simply that I couldn't see it anymore. I thought the wind must've picked up. I was looking directly into it now, facing east, and even with the house providing some shelter it was cutting whip-sharp into my face, and the flying snow was crusting on my eyelashes faster than I could blink it away.

My next thought—as the moments passed and the light did not reappear—was that Adya must've put it out deliberately.

He had agreed to the plan too quickly; he had let me go too easily. He hadn't wanted to use the pistol on me, perhaps. He hadn't wanted to waste the round, or he hadn't wanted to wake Vitya with the gunshot.

Or he couldn't bring himself to do it with his own two hands after all. This is a peculiarity I've noticed: that there are men who find it too distasteful to kill a woman even when they have no qualms about otherwise misusing her, or about killing a man. But Adya could let me go out into the storm, and he could do his best to ensure that I wouldn't find my way back.

I wasn't really afraid even then. I was not in immediate danger. I could spend the night in the woodshed, and I probably wouldn't freeze, and in the morning I could try for the Kaplans' farm or for the village.

But I was frustrated with myself. That I hadn't once considered this possibility, that I hadn't once wondered why Adya might've changed his mind and accepted my offer so readily, that I'd been so quick to show him what was under the loose stone after all. Clearly, he thought he didn't need me now.

And then, through the gusting snow, I saw him open the kitchen door, letting the warm yellow light of the stove flood out around him into the yard. He must've thrown open the grille and built up the fire as hot and bright as he could.

He stood there silhouetted against the firelight, waiting for me while I crossed back over. He took the rope from my unfeeling fingers and knelt without a word to tie it around the hitching post at the corner of the stoop. He took the logs from me and put them in the woodbin.

"Did you put out the lamp?" I asked him. My teeth were chattering. I hadn't felt cold in the yard, but now in the sudden heat of the stove, I couldn't stop shivering.

Adya kicked out the snow that had blown in, sweeping with the side of his boot, and shut the kitchen door. He started unbuttoning his coat, his frostbitten fingers moving slowly and carefully. "Take off your coat."

"Did you put out the lamp?"

"Why the hell would I put it out? The wind knocked it over. Take off your coat."

The lamp was in pieces on the stone floor. Spilled oil pooled in a slick puddle below the sink, gleaming wetly in the firelight. I took off my dripping coat, and Adya put his coat around my shoulders. I slipped my arms gratefully into the sleeves.

The coat was too big and smelled of him—of black earth and his sweat, sharp and sour, and faintly of old makhorka tobacco and cigarette smoke—but it was warm with his warmth and dry, and the wool was worn very soft. Adya took my coat and spread it out on the hearth before the stove.

It was the first time I'd seen him without his coat, and I realized that I had indeed missed something else about him besides his pocketknife: There were lieutenant's boards on the shoulders of his uniform tunic. He was wearing an ordinary enlisted man's coat—perhaps deceitfully, or perhaps for the same reason I wore a dead Austrian boy's coat—but he too was an officer.

I wondered why he hadn't taken off his shoulder boards as Vitya had. The boy was clearly highborn, there was no hiding it, but Adya might easily have passed as a conscript and spared himself a rigorous interrogation.

Vitya was awake now, sitting against the wall beside the stove, twisting the bottle of krupnik absently in his hands. Looking at me, looking at the bow saw.

He watched me sterilize the saw blade and Adya's knife and my bone needle and a length of thread pulled from the hem of my dress, all in boiled snow in a basting pan on the stovetop. His thin, young face was milk-pale even in the glow of the firelight.

"Adya says you do this in the hospital," he said.

"Yes—in the surgery. I'm a doctor's assistant."

His hands were clenched tightly on the bottle of krupnik. "It's unusual, isn't it? To be a girl working in the surgery?"

"Not as unusual as it was before the war."

"Yes, that's true," he said. And then: "What's your name?"

"Renia," I told him. The familiar form of my name—the only name I use now. I haven't introduced myself formally, as Countess Renata Krystyna Zamoyska of the Jelita coat of arms, for a very long time.

"I'm Vitya," he said.

"Yes, I know." I wondered how long it had been since he'd introduced himself by *his* full name and title. I knew he must have a title, though I didn't know then that he was Wiktor Witkowski—Viktor Vitkovsky to the Russians—great-grandson of the powerful and hated Kalikst Witkowski, whose nobility had been confirmed by Tsar Alexander II, the present tsar's grandfather.

We have all found, as I've said, that our names and titles mean very little in this war. His title hadn't stopped that bullet or this bacterial infection any more than mine had stopped the Russians who came to the house in June.

"It's something you do every day in the surgery, isn't it?" Vitya asked. His solemn dark eyes were on the blade again. "Just routine."

"Yes," I said.

I didn't tell him that in the surgery we use a specialized blade, much finer and sharper than the gap-toothed blade of that bow saw.

I didn't tell him that the operating theater is a clean, well-lighted room, and that—though I've operated several times by necessity without Doctor von Brenner's supervision—I had never once operated at night by firelight.

I didn't tell him that the patients are anesthetized first with laudanum or morphine or ether. And I did not tell him that one in twenty die even so.

I looked at Adya across the kitchen. He was filling in the crevice above the sink again, shutting out the draft. He met my eyes and looked away.

"Drink, Vitya," he said.

It was too dark without the lamp to work at the tabletop, so I sprinkled ashes over the hearth and covered them with pieces of old newspaper to absorb the blood.

When we had gotten Vitya to lie back on the newspaper with his leg outstretched, bare to the knee, a towel tied about his thigh as a tourniquet, Adya said low and tight into my ear, "I'm going to do it."

"You've got to hold him down. I can't."

"He weighs two kilos. You can hold him. You'd have to be the one bracing his leg anyway."

This was true, of course. We had only two sets of hands. If Adya were holding the boy's leg for me, the boy's hands would be free. I would've had to hold the leg and make the cut at the same time. It hadn't occurred to me because I'd never before operated on a patient without anesthesia.

I gave Adya his knife.

"Below the knee," I said to him. "You'll need to make incisions in the flesh first. Twelve centimeters below the kneecap in front, eighteen centimeters behind—enough so that the skin and muscles can be closed up over the bone afterward and sutured together, do you see?"

He nodded once, but I could see in his face that he was

already reconsidering. It's one thing to know theoretically that an amputation must be performed and quite another to take a blade to another human being's flesh.

He spent a moment holding the knife gingerly, staring at the blade in the firelight as if he'd never really seen it before, while I picked out a stick from the woodpile for Vitya to hold between his teeth. I thought I would have to take the knife away from Adya and do it myself after all. I didn't want the boy to see him hesitating. If he was going to lose his nerve, it was better if he lost it now and not in the middle of the operation.

But then, slowly, his shoulders very straight, he knelt beside Vitya on the newspaper and put his left hand on the boy's knee. His hands were calm and steady. He set the edge of the blade carefully against the pale skin, a hand's breadth below the kneecap. Vitya jerked a little.

"It's too high—you've got it too high. Adya—wait, Adya—"

Adya looked up at me without a word. His jaw was clenched.

"We need to do it right below the knee," I repeated to him quietly.

"No, please—just the foot." Vitya's voice was thin and sharp with panic and with krupnik. "Please, just the foot. Please, Adya. It's getting better. You said it's getting better. Please. You said."

I understood, of course. There is, apart from the medical risk, a social stigma that comes with amputation, with the more unsightly scars of war. Born of our own shame, perhaps. We dislike being reminded that the true face of war is often ignoble and always unromantic. To Vitya's panicking mind, the loss of a foot was more bearable than the loss of the entire lower leg, even if he would need a crutch or a prosthetic in either case.

I said calmly, "This type of gangrene—the infection may have spread without presenting visible symptoms yet." You all can appreciate, I'm sure, how callous it sounds to speak academically at a time like that, to speak from an emotional distance, but it's how we're trained to speak to a panicking patient. "We need to be sure we're removing all of it."

"I can't," Vitya said, "I can't, Adya. If it's just the foot—but I can't. Not the leg. Please, not the leg. Not the leg. You said it's getting better."

"Hold him," Adya said to me.

"No," Vitya gasped, jerking against my hands, "no, no, Adya, please. Not the leg. Please don't—please don't—"

"Bite the stick."

"Please don't—please—"

"Bite the fucking stick, Witek."

He used, in that moment, the Polish familiar form of the name. I didn't notice it then, but I recalled it later.

The boy got his arms free—it was, in hindsight, foolish of us to think I'd be able to hold him—and lunged up. Quick as a flash, Adya's left fist flew out and connected squarely with Vitya's jaw.

The boy's head snapped back. He flopped back down senseless on the newspaper.

"Suka," Adya cursed viciously, "*suka.*" And he kept on saying it to himself, low and tight and furious, while he made the incisions below the boy's knee, holding the calf under his hand and dissecting the flesh in swift, vengeful strokes.

I'll spare you the minutiae—

**"Oh, thank God for that, at least," Captain Baran mutters. He's looking rather green.**

I tied off the artery with a length of thread; Adya cut through the bone with the saw. Then he flung the saw savagely across the floor, gathered up the excised limb in bloody newspaper, and carried it out to the yard while I busied myself with the necessary remaining ligatures.

He was back in from the cold very soon; I was of course still wearing his coat. He had washed the blood from his hands in the snow. Without a word to me, he wiped snow from his face and came over to sit by Vitya. He slung his arm tight around the boy's shoulders while I folded up the loose flesh over the tibia and fibula and sutured it and rinsed it all with boiled salt water and dressed the stump.

Adya was asleep by the time I finished. Vitya was still unconscious. I put Adya's coat over both of them, washed my hands with the last of the warm salt water in the cooking pot, then emptied the pot into the yard and rinsed it with clean snow. That done, I crept across the room with my coat to sleep in the corner between the sink and the cellar door—only for a few minutes, I thought. I wanted to keep a close eye on that knee to make sure I'd gotten the bleeding stopped.

I'm not sure how long I slept, except that it must've been hours. When I woke up at last in the pitch dark, the stove had gone out. I had forgotten—and I think Adya had too—that we were supposed to be taking shifts.

# CHAPTER 9

I apologize if this is all rather shocking to you.

My entire world for the past four months has been the hospital, where, by necessity, we have all gotten used to such things and must treat them matter-of-factly. The sight of blood does not bother me anymore. I do not have the luxury of letting it bother me. I am keenly aware that very often my patients' lives depend on my ability to remain coolheaded under pressure and to do my work without qualm or hesitation.

It was my mother's wish that I should pursue a course of study at the medical university. She was not an overtly affectionate or sentimental woman—not, as I've said, the softhearted one of my parents. But she was duty bound. She felt very strongly that it was her responsibility as szlachcianka to be involved in the functions of the village, particularly in acts of charity and service, in visitation, in tending the sick and bedridden. She considered the study of medicine important to this end. She hadn't had the opportunity to attend university herself as a young woman, and she wished very much for me to have it.

I was not the first woman to attend the medical university, as women have been admitted to all imperial universities for fifteen years now, but I think I am the first of my rank. This didn't trouble my mother. She didn't care very much about appearances—at least, not merely for appearances' sake. She didn't go with me to Vienna when I was presented at court in January of 1914, the occasion of my official coming out in society, as she was busy assisting with a case of puerperal fever in the village. There was no question in her mind which was more important.

Of course then the war came, and the occupation, and everything that followed, and I gave no more thought to the university until this past summer, in July, when I was in hospital myself. Someone had come across the paperwork for my original application, it seems, when they were looking up my medical records, and one way or another my application ended up in Doctor von Brenner's hands.

I suppose it caught his eye that I had applied to the college of pediatrics, as he is a pediatrician himself by training. He came around to ask whether I was still interested in that course of study. I told him very frankly that I couldn't afford the tuition now, to which he replied that perhaps we could make an arrangement: I could attend classes for free in exchange for assisting him in the surgery.

As it turned out, I attended a total of just six class meetings before my work in the surgery overran everything else.

I admit that I accepted Doctor von Brenner's offer only because I saw very few other options, having just received the news about Emi. Besides, it seemed selfish to turn down the opportunity when it had dropped so unexpectedly into my lap, especially when my mother had wanted such an opportunity so badly and never got it. I am not sure I shared her sense of duty as szlachcianka. I knew by then how little my title means.

But I am very glad that I did take it, after all. The rest of my life may have turned upside down, but there is, I've found, a reassuring clarity and consistency to medical work. A gangrenous wound will always be a gangrenous wound, nothing more or less. I will always know what to do with it. When I fail, there will always be a scientific reason why. I find it comforting.

It was, I think, three or four o'clock in the morning when I woke, though of course in that pitch dark I couldn't tell for sure. The storm was still blowing fiercely; there would be no sunrise. I woke because I heard Vitya wake—that is, I heard him being sick on the floor.

It was breathtakingly cold, the bone-deep sort of cold that takes hours to thaw out, and in my haste to cross the room and relight the stove I very nearly wasted our last match because my hands were shaking so.

Vitya was not yet fully conscious. He was sitting up dazedly under Adya's arm, thickheaded with the combined effects of the alcohol and that blow to his face, which I am sure he did not remember. The marks of Adya's knuckles had blossomed into deep purple bruising along his jaw.

He blinked at me in the rekindled firelight in a feverish, uncertain sort of way. I do not think he remembered me just then, but he was unafraid. He was, above all, deeply ashamed of being sick.

"I'm sorry," he told me, "I'm sorry, I'll clean it"—and then he actually tried to get up, pushing Adya's coat off himself. Of course when he shifted the coat, he caught sight of the bandaged stump of his knee.

He was immediately sick again—sick from sheer reflex, sick with the shock. He leaned over and retched drily, in long, sobbing gasps, his lips dribbling feeble strings of saliva, his whole body shuddering with the effort to bring up something from his empty stomach.

Adya, awake all at once, held him by the shoulders and said to me tightly, "Krupnik."

I mention this detail because—more than anything else that had so far surprised me about Adya—it gave me pause. I was surprised that he knew to call it by that name.

That bottle was our own family recipe, unlabeled, and krupnik is not a Russian liqueur—and even here, as you know, it's primarily a luxury of the szlachta, the noble class. Not what a man like Adya, a commoner despite his military rank, would typically drink. But I supposed he could've come to know it if he'd served here during the occupation.

It was not a welcome thought. I'd stopped thinking of them as the enemy, but they were still Russian officers, and it was unpleasant to consider them in the context of the occupation or of the retreat. To consider whether they had perhaps been among those who came to Zarudce in June.

Of course that was highly unlikely. They might've been stationed anywhere. There was no reason to think they'd been in Lemberg even if they had been somewhere in the region of Galicia. Russian prisoners come to the Lemberg holding camp from hundreds of kilometers up and down the front, from as far north as Brześć in what was once Lithuania and as far south as Czernowitz on the Romanian border. And of course the Lemberg hospital is the collection point for most wounded prisoners, as the frontline hospitals do not have the resources to take them in.

But now, for the first time, I wondered. I wondered why they had come here, to this house, for shelter. I wondered why Adya had been so very sure the house was abandoned.

I didn't remember them. I felt certain I would remember their voices—if they had come to the house in June—even if I couldn't remember their faces. But I wondered.

There was perhaps a quarter of the bottle of krupnik left. We couldn't afford to waste a drop. I poured just a little into my tin cup and brought it over to Adya.

"Slowly," I told him.

"Drink, Vitya," Adya said, holding the cup to the boy's lips and tipping it carefully. The boy gasped and swallowed and almost immediately spat the stuff back up. Adya held the empty cup back up to me, shaking it impatiently when I made no move to take it.

I said, "No. We need to ration it."

"He needs it now. Give me the bottle."

"He can't keep it down."

"Give me the fucking bottle."

"We need to ration it," I repeated calmly, though I was holding on very tightly to the neck of the bottle behind my back, and my heart was pounding.

I couldn't stop thinking about it now—what if he had been here in June, what if he'd been one of the ones who came to the house, or what if he'd been one of the ones torching our fields or rustling off our milk cow while the rest dealt with me? What if that was why he'd presumed the house was empty now?

"We've only got a little bit left. And it isn't doing him any good now. He's still in shock. The pain will be worse when the shock has worn off."

Adya was silent, looking up at me. He was tensed like a

spring, ready to uncoil and leap up at me. I could see him turning each thought over in his head—that he could take the bottle away from me by force, I wouldn't be able to stop him, and he had very little reason to trust me after all—and setting each carefully aside in turn.

He said to me, half in concession, half in defiance, "Give him something to eat, then."

I cooked two slabs of bacon over the stove and cut up one of the potatoes to fry in the grease. I knew Vitya wouldn't eat it, but I cooked it anyway. The leftover drippings went into my grease pot, which I set on the stovetop to melt. I could float the wick from the shattered lamp in the grease pot, and we would have another light besides the stove. I brought one piece of bacon and half the potato over to Vitya on a shingle of pine bark from the woodbin; I have no plates.

Adya held out his hand for the shingle and said, "Look, Vitya."

That poor, wretched boy couldn't have cared less about any of this. He was lying curled on the floor, his cheek pressed into the wadded bundle of Adya's coat. His shoulders shook silently. He was making a very great effort not to sob aloud.

It was clear to me that he was ashamed of his pain—ashamed to acknowledge it, I mean, especially in front of me, a stranger, a woman, presumably a commoner at that. I'd given him no reason at all to suppose I was a noblewoman; one can certainly not tell by my hands anymore. At any rate, I could see that he was not going to lift his face from Adya's coat while I stood there watching.

I understood, of course. I too was brought up never to reveal any sort of weakness—certainly never to cry while anyone might be watching.

I took the other piece of bacon and the rest of the potato and sat in my corner between the sink and the cellar door to eat, affording him as much privacy as I could.

I wondered, as I sat there in my corner and listened to Adya try in vain to coax the boy into eating, whether this had fallen to me as a sort of penance—that it should turn out they had been here on that day last June. I don't remember for certain which day it was. I didn't put the date on Mieszko's headstone, as I couldn't afford the cost of the engraving at the time.

**Colonel Sosnkowski's brow is furrowed. "A point of clarification, Countess—by Mieszko, you mean young Count Zamoyski."**

**"My brother, Mieczysław Krystian—yes, Colonel. We called him Mieszko."**

**"You mean to say he died there—in Zarudce."**

**"Yes, Colonel. They killed him at the house on the day the retreat began."**

**Colonel Sosnkowski consults his own notes, laid out in neat piles on the tabletop before him. "There must be some mistake. Your brother served with General von Brudermann? According to our records, he died in Russian captivity in . . . November of 1914, in the Sretensk prisoner of war camp."**

**"You're thinking of my father, Colonel. He was the one at Sretensk. His name was also Mieczysław, and they both served under General von Brudermann in Lemberg, and they were both taken prisoner when the city fell. I believe that's where the mistake must've arisen. My father was on the general's staff. My brother was a lieutenant of infantry with the Thirtieth Division."**

**"I see. I knew they both served. I must've assumed they**

both died that first winter, perhaps because I knew that your mother—forgive me, Countess . . ." Colonel Sosnkowski has not once stumbled over his words until now. "I knew that your mother took her own life."

"Yes. In December, after we received word about my father. There had been a typhus outbreak in the prison camp."

My mother had preferred to join my father in death rather than live under the Russian occupation that had taken him from her. I'm not sure I expected it, but all the same it did not surprise me, and I do not blame her.

She was not a sentimental woman, at least not in the way it is usually meant; some might've called her cold. She had been suffering from melancholia for some time even before the war and was receiving clinical treatment for it. This I knew. But she was also a patriot, and she loved my father very much. I am not sure I realized how much until I found her body that morning. She had gone up into her apple orchard with one of his pistols, and she was holding his photograph in a little pocket frame in her hand.

It is traditional, of course, to withhold a Catholic burial after a suicide, given that it's considered a mortal sin, that the deceased acted out of faithless despair and took into her own hands God's prerogative of life and death. Father Urban wouldn't have refused us, gracious as he is. But to spare him any disciplinary action that might've come about as a result, we buried my mother where I had found her body, among her beloved apple trees on the hill above the house, rather than in the churchyard.

Of course the Russians cut down every one of those trees six months later, but I buried Mieszko there too just the same. The stumps remain. Perhaps one day they will grow and flower again.

"Your brother was not sent to the Sretensk camp?" Colonel Sosnkowski inquires.

"He was very badly wounded when the city fell, Colonel. He lost the use of his legs. General Brusilov permitted him to convalesce in Zarudce under house arrest."

"Then—forgive me for speaking bluntly, Countess, on what must be a very painful subject—presumably he was not killed on General Brusilov's orders. Presumably the killing was unsanctioned, perhaps even random."

"Presumably, yes. But they were General Brusilov's men who came to the house."

# CHAPTER 10

I should take the opportunity here to explain General Brusilov's clemency to Mieszko, as I do not want there to be any question whatsoever about Mieszko's loyalty.

He was, at twenty, one of the youngest graduates ever of the war college in Vienna. You met him in Kraków, Colonel Sosnkowski, so you know how exemplary his record was and how fine a soldier he made. He took a first lieutenant's commission in General von Brudermann's army here in Lemberg when the war began and was largely responsible for holding the line so that the general and most of his staff could escape when the city fell to the Russians in early September. In the process, he was badly wounded and could not evacuate.

My father, who had safely crossed the San River with General von Brudermann, went back for his son with a small relief force and ended up captured himself. I am not sure whether that was bravery or foolishness. Had he succeeded, it would've been bravery.

Of course officers are typically given preferential treatment in captivity. This is as true when the Russians take prisoners as it is when we take prisoners. There is a certain old-fashioned sense of chivalry about it; officers are, for instance, permitted to keep their swords. In the old days, the idea was that an officer, as a nobleman, could be held for ransom and therefore shouldn't be mistreated, as the condition of the prisoner would affect the amount of prize money that could be demanded.

Individual officers are not usually ransomed these days, but all the same, they receive privileges and considerations that are not afforded to captive enlisted men. I'm told that after the fall of Przemyśl, the Russians allowed captive officers to take eighty-two kilograms of luggage apiece into captivity, and paid them a respectable salary in rubles each month so that they would not be forced to work, and permitted them to contact their families by way of telegraph messages. This is in quite some contrast, I understand, to their treatment of enlisted men, who are subject to floggings and beatings even for minor infractions and shipped off to forced labor in the mines or on the railways of distant, frozen Siberia.

So it is not unheard of for badly wounded officers to be allowed time to convalesce before they are sent into captivity. But that is not why Mieszko was permitted to remain in Zarudce. Or not the only reason.

He had come to General Brusilov's attention, it seems, because he refused to be separated from his soldiers. They are typically housed separately, captive officers and enlisted men, for the reasons I've stated, but Mieszko remained with his men. He would not even accept medical treatment for himself until his most badly wounded men had been seen to, regardless of their rank.

I do think General Brusilov was impressed. I do think he felt a genuine respect for Mieszko's conduct. But most of all I think he viewed Mieszko as dangerous.

I think he was worried about the effect Mieszko might have—on the enlisted men and on the other officers. I think he was worried that Mieszko might inspire rebelliousness in his fellow prisoners. I think Mieszko was kept in Zarudce because General Brusilov felt it was risky to send him off into captivity. Caution masked as kindness. The Russian fear of Polish rebelliousness is deep-seated, as you all know—and not without reason, I suppose, given the history of uprisings in Russian-ruled Poland.

In any case, Mieszko did not take it as kindness. This all came about in the first place because he wished to be with his men. He felt guilty to be left here at home; he felt he had betrayed them. And it is hard for *me* to take it as kindness, even if General Brusilov didn't order him killed.

Because if he hadn't been at home in Zarudce on that morning in June, if he'd been with his men in captivity as he wished to be, it is quite possible he would still be alive.

Vitya lost consciousness again. The shock of the amputation was of course taking a great toll upon his ravaged, malnourished body, and he had no way to build up his reserves again as he could keep nothing in his stomach.

It must've been, by now, about five o'clock in the morning—this was last Saturday, the first morning of our Roman Catholic new year, though no one was thinking of that in the moment.

Adya got up stiffly and went down into the cellar to relieve himself. When he came back up, he sat beside Vitya against the wall and ate the bacon and potatoes off the shingle.

It was a silent admission of defeat. We both knew at that point that the boy was going to die.

I looked closely now at Adya's shoulder boards. They bore the number *19* embroidered in metallic thread. I didn't know enough about the Russians' unit composition to know whether the Nineteenth Division had been part of General Brusilov's Twelfth Army Corps in Lemberg.

I said to him, "Were you stationed in Lemberg?"

He looked up sharply. He had been somewhere very far away. "What?"

"Were you with General Brusilov in Lemberg?"

He didn't answer. He was eating the pieces of potato unhurriedly, one by one, chewing each piece thoroughly and swallowing before he moved on to the next, as though giving himself time to reflect upon it.

"I thought you might've been stationed in Lemberg," I said carefully, "because you knew it was krupnik—"

"Save it," he said. "I'm not a fool, and neither are you. Say what you want to say."

"You knew this house."

"Yes."

"You knew what happened here. You thought the house would be empty."

"Yes."

"Were you here?" I asked him. "That morning?"

"I didn't ask you to stay," he said. "I didn't ask you to help."

"Were you here in June?"

"I wasn't in Zarudce. Why the hell does it matter? Do you think it only happened in Zarudce? We burned every farm larger than ten morgens between here and Łuck."

"But you knew this house," I said.

He finished his last mouthful of potato, licked the grease from his fingers, and leaned his head back against the wall.

"I heard a story," he said. "From a corporal in Twelfth Division. He said they'd been through Zarudce during the retreat. He said they'd killed the szlachcic's son when they burned the manor. I didn't think about it again until I saw the house yesterday. Vitya needed to stop—that's all I was thinking. I didn't know you would be here. I didn't think anyone would be here. I wouldn't have stopped if I'd known."

"He would've been dead last night if you hadn't stopped," I said.

I suppose it was odd that I was the one trying to comfort him in that moment. I suppose it's a habit of mine at this point. In so many ways, women are trained to put aside their own grief and think first of the grief of others. But it would've done nothing for my wounds to salt his, and truly I was offering small comfort anyway.

Adya let out an ugly little breath of a laugh and said, "So I bought him eight hours."

All told, it was about twelve hours. The boy woke up only once more—around eight o'clock, I think—and only long enough to call out in a disoriented panic for Adya. He was unconscious again by the time Adya leaned over him. We couldn't wake him after that. We couldn't bring his fever down. I believe he had gone into septic shock, and there was very little we could've done for him at that point even if we had been able to get him to the hospital.

He died almost exactly at noon. I was holding his wrist and using Leo Adamczyk's pocket watch to time his pulse. I felt his heart stop.

Adya had been sitting there with his arm about the boy's shoulders ever since Vitya had woken earlier. He laid Vitya down flat on the floor now and felt the pulse and heartbeat for himself.

He crouched there on his heels for a moment, his palm resting on the boy's chest. Then he crossed himself, gathered up the boy's body very gently, and carried him down into the cellar.

He crossed himself from left to right. I thought nothing of it in the moment because it's the way I cross myself, the way all Catholics of the Roman rite cross themselves. There was nothing unusual about it to my mind.

It didn't occur to me until later, when I returned Leo Adamczyk's watch to its box and caught sight of his rosary and prayer book there, that Russians cross themselves from right to left. That is the Orthodox way and also, I believe, the Greek Catholic way.

I had missed many things about Adya, and I had missed this too: He was not Russian. He was Polish.

# CHAPTER 11

It is midmorning now.

My testimony has gone on for nearly two hours, and Colonel Sosnkowski must sense that his audience is getting restless, because he interrupts me to announce a short recess. We're to reconvene in half an hour.

Chairs are scraped back; cigarette cases and matchboxes are produced; orderlies are dispatched for coffee and tea. I look for Lieutenant Kijek, but he has already been spirited away by his guards.

I don't know where they're keeping him. It's entirely possible that he, too, has been kept here at the manor house and they've just taken care not to let our paths cross over these past four days.

It wouldn't be difficult. Count Potocki's house is quite large, more in the style of a grand Viennese palace than the traditional Polish dwór; my house, which was the largest in Zarudce, feels very small and rustic in comparison. In addition to the parlor and the great room, the main floor of the Potocki house boasts a chapel, a billiards room, a drawing room, a writing room, the library, and several salons. There are two stories of bedrooms and dressing rooms besides, and of course the kitchens and servants' quarters. Quite enough space in which two people might exist for four days unseen by one another.

But I'm worried about Lieutenant Kijek just the same. I'm worried that he hasn't been shown quite the same considerations in his imprisonment that I've been shown in mine. He is an officer, yes, but he is also a commoner—and in any case he stands accused of espionage.

I ask, and am given permission, to take my daily walk. I doubt I'll have the need or opportunity come this afternoon. As usual, I take the path that goes past the stables and carriage house and paddock up to the very top of the hill. Count Potocki's house, like mine, sits on a slope with the grounds falling away below. It has long been tradition to build the szlachcic's house on the high ground.

It's a cold, clear day, and the sun is shining very brightly. We haven't had temperatures above freezing since the storm, so the ground is still covered with a deep mantle of snow, except in the yard, which has been cleared by necessity to make way for motorcars. My guards follow me at a respectful distance, rifles slung at their backs. They accompany me anytime I leave my cell—two of them, both soldiers of His Highness the Archduke Joseph Ferdinand's Fourth Army like Captain Baran. I have a third attendant, a woman, who brings me my meals and anything else I need and takes care of my washing.

None of them speak to me. I assume they're under orders not to, and accordingly I do not speak to them as I don't wish to make things difficult for them. I haven't even asked their names. It is not appropriate for me to try to make friends of them. My circumstances are humiliating for all of us.

From the top of the hill—at least at this time of year when the trees are bare—one can see all of Lemberg in the distance. The Potocki estate sits nestled in the low hills just northwest of the city, and from here I can make out the triple spires of Saint Elizabeth's Church and the dome of Saint George's Cathedral and the clock tower at City Hall and the bell tower at the Dormition church, the steep wooded rise of the old High Castle grounds and the proud winged bronze statues to Glory, Poetry, and Music atop the pediment of the opera house.

I think I could sit up here on this old felled oak trunk forever, looking at the city spread out in frozen miniature below me like a tableau in a snow globe. I've seen Vienna now, and Kraków. Even so—even in wartime—I think Lemberg, Lwów in Polish, L'viv in Ukrainian, is the most beautiful city in all the empire, perhaps the world. Where else can one find a place so thoroughly Polish and Ukrainian, Austrian and Jewish all at once? The thought of leaving it for Emi's ancestral estate at Göllersdorf, had my marriage proceeded as planned, was wrenching, lovely though Göllersdorf was.

One of my guards, the senior of the two, a tall high-cheekboned boy of perhaps twenty with corporal's shoulder boards on his coat, approaches me rather cautiously, with a polite nod. He speaks to me in fluent Polish, which is a pleasant surprise. I assumed they were Austrians.

"If you please, Countess Zamoyska. We'd better start back."

Has it really been nearly half an hour? I've lost track of the time. That's unusual for me. I have, by long practice and necessity, developed a very keen sense of timing. But of course I'm moving more slowly these days on account of my rib, and I think it's thrown me off.

"Yes, of course," I say.

If we are making a list of my weaknesses of character: How selfish I had been, how shortsighted, to wish I wouldn't have to leave Lemberg. Now, I would leave it behind me in a heartbeat, if only it would bring Emi back to me.

Beyond seven mountains, beyond seven forests, there was a cold, proud queen of a lonely island realm who was unlucky enough to catch the eye of Kościej, the evil king of the underworld.

Determined to have her for his own, but unable to force her—as she had the power to turn him to ice with her glance—furious Kościej laid siege to the island, cast a spell of deathlike sleep over all its inhabitants, and imprisoned the queen alone in her own castle, guarded by a dragon, until she should agree to surrender herself to him.

She herself, the only one of her people left alive, could do nothing but wander her empty halls grief-stricken, praying to the clouds and the wind and the stars and the moon and the sun that the handsome knight of whom she had long been dreaming would come to her rescue.

Days passed, then weeks, then months, then years. Her empty castle crumbled into ruins. Her soldiers lay where they fell in the field below the castle walls, their armor slowly turning to rust. And then, just when the queen had given up all hope, her hero knight appeared at last.

He had spent all this time carefully learning from the old witch Baba Jędza the secret of killing Kościej. Had he tried to come to the queen's rescue at once, without heeding Jędza, no doubt Kościej would've easily killed him instead.

I suppose there's a good lesson there. I suppose it teaches us the importance of patience, and the mystery of providence—that the divine is at work even and perhaps especially when we cannot see it. But her knight does come for her at last, and he does kill Kościej. The queen's patience is rewarded. All her pain and sorrow are forgotten; all her dead are returned to life. There is somehow a priest on hand to celebrate the marriage sacrament, and then there is a joyous wedding feast that continues long into the night.

There are no tales that I can recall in which the queen succumbs quietly to her grief because her knight has been killed by the Russians before the walls of Przemyśl. Sometimes I think we could use those lessons too.

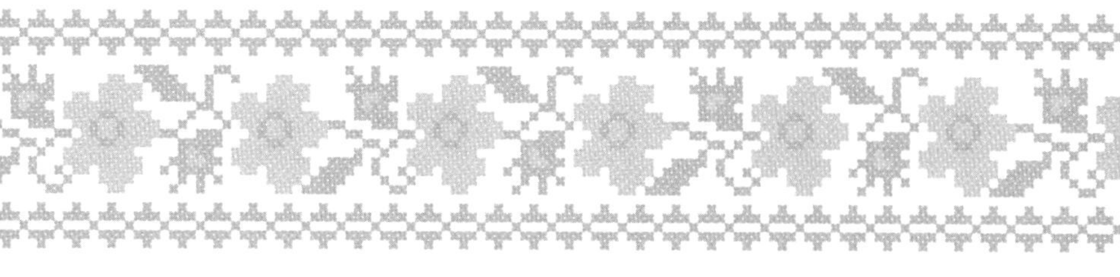

# CHAPTER 12

I was explaining that I had realized Lieutenant Kijek was Polish.

**He's returned to his seat at the back of the room. I didn't turn to see them bring him in, but I heard them. I knew it was him because at one point he tripped or was shoved, and when he stumbled he said, "Kurwa," and I recognized his voice.**

It seems so obvious now. It seems so very improbable that in nearly twenty-four hours I had never once suspected that the lieutenant was Polish. That both of them, as I would come to learn, were ethnic Poles, not Russians. I am Polish, after all; surely I should've guessed.

I imagine you think there were ways to tell. Clues I missed, perhaps, even before Adya let slip that he knew to call it krupnik or spoke the boy's name in Polish in a moment of stress. And perhaps there were.

But then, too, perhaps you forget that we'd been speaking Russian that whole time, and Adya's was fluent enough to sound native to my ear. Which makes sense, as Russian was the official language of Privislinsky Krai, the Vistula Land, the part of the old Polish-Lithuanian Commonwealth subjected to Russian rule until last September. He would've grown up speaking Russian. It was forbidden, as I understand, for the Poles of the Vistula Land to speak or write in their own language—one of the punishments meted out by the Russian authorities in retribution for the failed January Uprising of fifty years ago.

Kalikst Witkowski, Vitya's great-grandfather, made his name in that uprising. He was head of the so-called Investigative Committee interrogating and executing captured Polish patriots in the Pawiak prison in Warsaw, and he did his job with such bloodthirsty zeal that the Russians entrusted him with the presidency of the city—a rare honor, as most of the presidents before and since were ethnic Russians, not Poles.

It's little wonder that Vitya took care not to reveal his name to me. Even here in Austrian-ruled Lemberg, as you know, Poles are likely to spit when they hear the name Witkowski.

So I knew only to call them as they called each other—Adya and Vitya. I knew only that "Adya" was the Russian familiar form of the name Adrian, which itself may be either Russian or Polish. I did not know his surname. Kijek is quite clearly a Polish surname, not a Russian one.

But of course we like to think that we know our own—that we know when one is ours or theirs, that the differences are plain, that there are always signs and clues if one pays close enough attention. We like to think we can always clearly tell Polish or German or Russian or Austrian, enemy or friend. It's unsettling, and damaging to our pride, to admit that sometimes we can't. That sometimes we are all very much the same apart from the uniform.

Captain Baran lets out a derisive snort and says, "Whore. Is she trying to justify lifting her skirt for him?"

He's speaking German, but the word sounds near enough in German and Polish, and from the back of the room Lieutenant Kijek snarls at him, "Kutas"—which does not sound like the German but which requires no translation regardless.

"It's a wieśniak's name, Kijek," says Captain Baran loudly, in Polish for the lieutenant's benefit. "A peasant's name, an illiterate's name . . ."

"Baran is a sheep-fucker's name," says Lieutenant Kijek.

"For the love of Christ, one more word from either of you"—Colonel Sosnkowski, also in Polish—"and I'll have you taken out and shot right now."

I'm not sure how many people in this room know even as much as I know about Colonel Sosnkowski, about the sort of work he's rumored to do for the Organizacja Wojskowa. But everyone seems to have accepted that he's not a man to be underestimated. In any case, neither Captain Baran nor Lieutenant Kijek is fool enough to test whether he really means the threat.

The captain, halfway to his feet, resumes his seat in stiff silence. He doesn't look at me. He hasn't looked at me or spoken to me directly since the arrest.

I'm sorry for his sake that it had to come to this. He was close to Mieszko during their time together at the war college in Vienna. He was one of a very small number of officer candidates not to come from the old imperial aristocracy, and I imagine most of his classmates never let him forget it. Mieszko—firm in his socialist convictions even then, always conscious of an injustice and cheerfully unbothered by anyone else's opinion—befriended him their first week in the barracks.

I doubt the captain will ever forgive me for betraying Mieszko's memory, try as I might to explain myself.

There are other casualties of war besides the dead—something else Mieszko wrote to me in his anger and frustration after the rout at the Gniła Lipa. I didn't understand him then, but I do now.

Captain Sosnkowski says, in German now, slowly, "Would you say, Countess, that you felt compelled to aid Lieutenant Kijek because you knew he was also Polish?"

"At this point, you mean."

"Yes. Regardless of your actions toward Captain Witkowski, which, as we have established, are not the reason you were arrested. Did you at this point continue providing aid to Lieutenant Kijek because you knew now that he was Polish, not Russian?"

He's extending another kindness to me, as a life preserver is extended to a drowning man. A way to save myself.

This is of course a German tribunal; my fate is in General von Linsingen's hands. But Commandant Piłsudski has von Linsingen's ear and enjoys his great respect, and Commandant Piłsudski is not just a Pole but a nationalist. He fights for a sovereign and unified Poland, a free Poland—the Poland that my father, lying in some unmarked shallow grave in Siberia, will never get to see, nor my mother and Mieszko in the ruined earth that was once our apple orchard. And am I not a patriot too, like them?

It would be easy to say yes, of course—yes, I sacrificed my honor and disrupted the war effort for the lieutenant because we share the same Polish blood. That might win me the commandant's favor and von Linsingen's clemency. But it would not be the truth.

**I am a patriot. I will go to my death with a prayer for free Poland on my lips. But if I am to die, I wish to set this part of the record straight.**

**"No, Colonel."**

**"It didn't influence your actions in any way—to know the lieutenant was Polish?"**

**"No. I would've done the same if he were Russian, or German, or Austrian. His blood doesn't matter. I would've done what I did because I couldn't live with myself otherwise."**

I cleaned the boy's blood from the knife and the saw. I didn't want Adya to have to do it. He put on his coat and went to get more wood from the shed—at least, he brought more wood when he came back. He didn't speak of Vitya. It was as if a door had been shut and locked.

He piled the wood into the bin and said to me, pulling his scarf from his mouth, "Is that all you've got—what's in the shed?" The strip of exposed skin on his face was red with windburn. His eyes were streaming but not, I think, from the wind.

He spoke in Russian still. He'd had his back to me when he made his prayer over the boy's body. He didn't know that I'd watched him cross himself, and I didn't tell him, just as I didn't tell him now that I could see he'd been crying. I answered him in Russian.

"Yes, that's all." The Kaplan boy generally keeps the woodshed full for me, as I've said, but he had been in bed with a chill since Wednesday morning, and I hadn't had time to split more wood myself.

"It'll be gone tonight if the stove stays lit," Adya said. "Maybe the morning."

"Perhaps the storm will break," I said.

He said nothing. It was stilted and awkward now—to talk to him across the gulf of the boy's death. Urgency and necessity had brought us very close for a brief time; now we had moved apart again.

He sat down heavily against the wall beside the stove, dropping his head back, and started unbuttoning his coat. He worked very slowly, rubbing his hands in the intervals as he moved from button to button, fingers stiff and fumbling. The frostbite had begun to welt into angry red blisters.

I said, "Don't rub it. Let it blister."

"It hurts." He sounded tired and very young. It was a childlike thing to say. I'd forgotten that he was not, after all, very much older than Vitya. Or me.

"It will hurt worse if you break the blisters." I held out a hand. "Let me see it."

"Leave it."

"Then let me see the wound."

He stiffened.

"You've been running a fever since last night at least. It's infected, whatever it is. We need to treat it now, while the symptoms are still mild."

"It's from this." He indicated his blistered fingers impatiently.

"You don't run a fever from frostbite. Unless it's become infected, in which case I'd better see it."

He was silent, working at his coat buttons. He shrugged off the coat with some effort and started on the buttons of his uniform tunic. He didn't protest when I sat down beside him, moved his hands away, and unbuttoned the placket of the tunic for him. It was the standard Russian service tunic, the gymnastyorka, which has no front opening and must be lifted off over the head, and he drew a low, careful breath as he raised his right arm. I pulled the tunic away. He rolled up the thin, loose sleeve of his undershirt to show me.

There was a soiled strip of rough Hessian cloth, crusted stiff and black with old blood, wrapped inexpertly about his forearm. In the half-light, holding his arm across my lap as I unwound the cloth, I thought he had somehow managed to mangle the arm on barbed wire.

Then, as I peeled more of that filthy cloth away, brushing gently at the dirt and dried blood, I realized that the marks were from a blade, not a wire. Someone had, with deliberation, cut the word *RUSEK* in crude Latin capitals deeply into the flesh on the inside of his forearm, from wrist to elbow.

It had been done with a bayonet, not a kit knife, judging by the breadth of the lacerations. It had been done very recently; the infection was young.

It is, of course, a distinctively Polish slur for Russians, *rusek*. It was clear to me that this had been done to him by Poles—by ethnic Poles, that is, rather than by Ukrainians or others who might serve in so-called Polish battalions but who have their own particular words for the enemy.

I've learned in the hospital never to ask, never to pry. I don't speak to my patients about what they've seen or done or endured at the front unless they indicate to me that they wish to speak about it. Many of them do; many don't or can't. But it shook me so—to see that ugly word cut into his flesh, to know one of his own people, my own people, must've done it—that I couldn't help myself.

"Why didn't you tell them?"

He was breathing carefully through his nostrils as I inspected his arm. The lacerations were swollen with infection, no doubt sore to the touch. "Tell what?"

“You’re Polish.”

He snorted. “Why the hell do you think they did it? I’m a Pole killing Poles for the tsar.”

**“Make a note here, if you please, Lieutenant,” Colonel Sosnkowski instructs the typist. “Countess Zamoyska’s assessment of the wound has been corroborated by a medical officer of the First Brigade of the Polish Legions. We are recommending disciplinary action to be taken against those responsible. Continue, Countess.”**

I boiled salt water on the stove and worked at the cuts until I had broken open the scabs again. Fresh blood would help flush out the infection. Then I reached for the bottle of krupnik and spent a little while turning his arm gingerly this way and that, rinsing it with krupnik and wiping it with a fold of my apron before the alcohol could run onto his blistered hands.

It hurt him. He didn’t flinch or groan, but he leaned his head back against the wall and started talking to distract himself.

“Two weeks ago,” he said, “the Nineteenth had orders to destroy Łąka. It was punitive. The other villages, we gave evacuation orders first. Łąka was different. The order came from division. The women and children went to the train in Rovno to be deported to labor camps. The men, all of them . . .”

“Yes,” I said, “we heard about Łąka.”

“They knew I was from the Nineteenth when they took us—Vitya and me,” he said. “They were Poles. I took off Vitya’s insignia before they searched us. I told them I was the ranking officer. Vitya was General Brusilov’s fucking aide-de-camp. If they’d known, they’d have put the bullet in his head, not in his ankle.”

I wrapped his arm with a clean dishcloth. I have no dressing gauze in the house. I said, "This is no more than five days old. Maybe less."

"They took us four days ago."

"Behind the lines?"

He was silent.

Because of course—as you know—it takes a week to reach the front from Lemberg, now that the train no longer runs any farther east than Sokal, on the old line to Łuck. I know this because I've been up to Sokal myself to coordinate the collection of wounded at the station there, where they arrive from the front by horse cart or on foot. In the winter, on treacherous mud roads, the trip takes a week at least.

If the Legions had taken him four days ago, they had taken him well behind our own lines.

I poured half of the remaining krupnik into my tin cup for him. I kept what was left in the bottle for myself. It's a fine, honey-sweet liqueur of clear pale gold, our krupnik. My father was always very proud of it.

Adya took the cup and tipped his krupnik back in one swift, practiced swallow, leaning his head against the wall. Then he set the cup down and let out that little breath of a laugh.

"They were my orders," he said. "I was supposed to do it—destroy Łąka. The orders came down from Brusilov himself, and division told my platoon to do it. Suka. I refused. They arrested me for insubordination and sent me up to headquarters in Rovno for a court-martial and a firing squad. Vitya broke me out. Threw away his rank and his title and his career. Saved my life. I was taking him home to Petrograd. He's a Witkowski—he *was* a Witkowski. He's got kin in Petrograd, and they've got the money to buy him a pardon or send him abroad or whatever the hell they need to do. I was trying to take him home. I didn't know we'd crossed the lines. They took us four days ago outside Beresteczko."

Something seemed to snap inside him all at once. He buried his face in his hands.

"I told him I'd get him home," he said. His voice came thick and rough through his blistered fingers. "I killed him."

And of course it was no use for me to try to convince him that the fault was not his. No more use than it would've been for him, or for anyone, to try to convince me that the fault for that hanged Ukrainian boy was not mine. It was no use trying to explain to him that clearly the gangrene had already spread much farther into the boy's body than the knee. Gas gangrene is so deadly precisely because it develops so quickly. The most skilled surgeon in the world couldn't have saved that boy's life.

So I did the only thing I could do for him, the only thing I can do in the hospital when my patients succumb under the weight of guilt and grief: I slipped my arms around his shoulders, and I held him while he cried.

# CHAPTER 13

Since you will ask: It did occur to me that he might be lying.

Not about Łąka, I mean—not about the massacre. I knew that was true because one of the survivors was brought to us at the hospital afterward. He was a boy of sixteen or so who had survived by playing dead beneath another fallen body after the Russians shot him. He was badly wounded but still had managed to crawl away on his belly after darkness fell and cross the river to our lines near Łuck.

My understanding—and I'm sure you all know better than I—is that the Legions had conducted a raid across the river in the vicinity of Łąka and had succeeded in killing or capturing a number of Russian officers, and the Russians believed that someone in the village had supplied the Legions with intelligence prior to the raid. I don't know whether Lieutenant Kijek was in fact the one ordered to carry out the punitive operation against Łąka afterward; I just knew that such an operation had taken place.

But if Lieutenant Kijek and Captain Witkowski had been making for Petrograd, as the lieutenant claimed, it seemed unlikely to me that they should've ended up in Beresteczko, which, as you know, is nearly due west from the Russian headquarters in Rovno. It seemed much more likely that they would've followed the Horyn River north from Rovno toward Minsk and thence either to the harbor at Riga or overland by way of Pskov. Lieutenant Kijek didn't strike me as the sort to blunder his way across enemy lines, quite in the wrong direction of where he intended to go.

But stranger things have happened in war. At night, on unfamiliar ground, with a narrow escape from execution just behind him—yes, I supposed it was possible that he had simply made a mistake and struck out west rather than north. Perhaps the sky had been overcast that night, or perhaps he had sidetracked to avoid a patrol, one of ours or one of their own. Not likely, but possible, and certainly the simplest explanation.

I think that was how I rationalized it to myself in the moment. It was simplest to believe that he was telling the truth, that he had stumbled to my door in Zarudce by sheer accident.

But of course I have no way to prove to you that I did not know he was a spy. And in any case—

**"He has been charged with espionage," Colonel Sosnkowski corrects mildly, with characteristic attention to accuracy. "He has not yet been convicted."**

**"Yes, Colonel. What I mean to say is that it makes no difference in any case."**

**"You mean you would've acted as you did regardless."**

**"I think I've made that clear, Colonel."**

**"Even knowing he was behind the lines as a spy for the Russians? Even knowing he had lied to you regarding his purpose and intentions?"**

**"He would still deserve a trial, Colonel. He would still deserve the chance to speak in his own defense."**

**"He will have it. We are not presuming his guilt."**

**"I acted as I did to guarantee him that chance, Colonel."**

Adya spent most of that second afternoon asleep in feverish exhaustion, slumped against the wall beside the stove. He had used up his own reserves, I think, holding himself together for four days in front of the boy. This was surrender.

I made good use of the time. I knotted together the cut bits of twine from Pani Adamczyk's parcel and hung up the empty feed sacks as a sort of privacy screen from the ceiling joist in the far corner of the room. I put the night pot there. We wouldn't need to use the cellar again while the boy lay down there. Then I took stock of everything we had available to us in our close little world of that kitchen.

Food was no concern. The bacon we would need to ration sparingly, but the potatoes and fish, in two good-sized portions, would've fed us for more than a week, and I couldn't imagine that the storm would last that long. We could use the cooking grease for lamp oil, and we could melt snow on the stove for drinking and washing up.

The most pressing concern was that stove. We had no more matches, no other way to light it if it went out again.

And it didn't matter, as it turned out, how much split wood we had left in the shed: We couldn't reach it now even by my lifeline. The wind must've shifted and started cutting across the yard. The snow had piled as high as the eaves of the roof against the kitchen stoop. I went to bring in another armful of wood, and I opened the kitchen door to face a solid white wall of drifted snow.

But we had plenty of other things to burn.

I managed, with some difficulty, to pry open the door to the ruined, empty great room. I hadn't opened it once since I sealed it off with rags and old newspaper for the winter, and the damp in the cracks around the jambs had long since gone to ice.

I took the hammer from the tool kit below the sink and set to work loosening the boards I had nailed across the broken windows last summer. I'd nailed them from the outside, which meant that from the inside now I couldn't just pry the nails out; I had to pound awkwardly at the boards until the nails finally shivered free of the masonry. Now and then the rotting boards simply shattered to bits under the hammer, and I had to work the splintered pieces off the nails by hand.

It wasn't hard work, just tedious. It was numbingly cold with the wind and snow gusting in through the newly opened gaps between the boards. And in truth it was difficult to be in that room again. Not just because of what happened there in June, but because of everything that happened before.

I have a great many fond memories of that room. The Christmas Eves of my childhood—the candlelit hours between our Wigilia and the Pasterka Mass at midnight, the supper dishes all cleared away and the gifts handed out. We would bundle into quilts before the tree and listen in rapt silence as my father told the stories of old Poland, of King Lech and the white eagle, of the dragon of Wawel Hill, of the knights asleep under Mount Giewont who will awaken in Poland's hour of greatest need.

And of course that one Sunday dinner of five years ago, when Mieszko was home on leave from the war college. The young Count Potocki was there too. I couldn't stand him, I'm sorry to say, and Mieszko must've been able to tell. They were seated next to each other at the table, and at one point Mieszko reached for a sauceboat and managed to upend the entire thing into young Potocki's lap. He did it so innocently and apologized so profusely that I thought it was an accident, until he winked at me across the table.

More than anything else, that room reminds me how much I've lost.

At any rate, I hadn't set foot in there since that morning in June. They killed Mieszko in there. They spent some time questioning him before they killed him, and they tied him to one of the dining chairs while they questioned him—at least, that's how I saw his body situated when they brought me in afterward, so that's how I presume it happened.

I wasn't there at first, you understand. I was down in the village to attend Pani Fedyk, who'd just given birth, and her eldest son, Andriy, had come racing in with the news that the Grand Duke Nicholas, the Russians' commander in chief, had ordered a general retreat from Galicia, as the Austro-Hungarian Sixth Corps under General Mackensen's command were within thirty kilometers of Lemberg.

I returned to the house at about eleven o'clock, at which point the Russians had already been there for some time, and Mieszko was dead.

I'm thankful for that. He didn't have to watch what they did to me. I'm not sure he could've borne it stoically as he had borne the rest—he had answered them not a word, it seems, which I imagine contributed to their frustration.

I don't dwell upon that morning. It does me no good to dwell upon it. In any case, I was brought up to believe that the best salve for grief and soul sickness is physical work, and I had work to do now.

You are from Warsaw, I believe, Colonel Sosnkowski; perhaps you too grew up listening to the story of the beautiful trickster goddess who on Saint John's Night would take the form of a golden duck in the dungeons below the old Ordynacki Palace on Tamka Street. If you could catch her in that form, she would give you a purse full of one hundred gold ducats and the promise of treasures untold, on one easy condition: You must spend every last one of those ducats on yourself within the span of one day.

And so—as my father told it—the hero of the story, a poor young shoemaker's apprentice named Ludek, caught the duck and took the purse and indulged himself in luxuries he'd only ever dreamed of: the choicest food and wine, the finest clothes, a smart horse-drawn carriage, a theater box.

Then finally, his day nearly done, he gave his last handful of ducats to an old soldier of Napoleon's army begging for alms outside the theater. The goddess appeared at once in a flash of lightning to scoff at him for spoiling his chance at a lifetime of wealth and happiness. But the old soldier told him, "It isn't a ducat, young master, that brings happiness, but an honest day's work."

It's rather conceited coming from me, I know—to say that true comfort and happiness are in the work of one's hands, when I never had to make a living with my own hands until this past year. But it's the moral of a great many of those old stories of my childhood, and I've done my best to take it to heart.

So I was busy at work, pulling with both hands at a splintered board, when Adya put his hand on mine, trying to take the board from me. He had come up silently behind me in the feeble half-light, his footfalls muffled by the drifted snow on the floor.

His touch was not rough or forceful. Quite the opposite. But it was unexpected. And though he was no taller than I, he was stronger, all lean bone and muscle, and he had in effect pinned me there between his body and the wall.

I reacted by reflex and memory. I turned on him, pushing him away from me as hard as I could, my fists striking sharply at his chest and gut, my knee between his legs; I couldn't help myself. He was lucky that I wasn't holding the hammer just then.

He went to his knees on the snowy floor with a choked sort of grunt, doubling over a little as though winded. I had hit him quite hard. He held his hands up, palms toward me, and I let out a shaking breath.

"Don't touch me. Please."

"Proszę wybaczyć, moja pani," he said.

He said it in Polish, and he said it quite formally—*wybaczyć*, as one is supposed to say to one's elders or betters; *moja pani*, my lady, as one of our villagers in Zarudce might've said deferentially to me once upon a time. It was jarringly old-fashioned, a relic of a time when a man like Adya would've hardly dared look at me, much less put a hand on me.

I said to him calmly, "You need to cover your hands." That was pride, equally old-fashioned—to carry on as though nothing had happened, to pretend he hadn't frightened me. He knew he had; he must've known why. If he'd heard what they did to the szlachcic's son, he must've heard what they did to the szlachcic's daughter.

But we both pretended. He went back into the kitchen without a word and wrapped up his frostbitten hands with strips of dishcloth, rather like Saint Lazarus wrapped in graveclothes. When he came back, he was careful to keep away from me, though always in my line of sight.

We worked in silence. He loosened the boards from the masonry for me, and I piled them together and carried them into the kitchen. When we'd stripped everything from the windows, I sealed off the door again, tightly.

We could've pulled up the floorboards too: The floor in the great room is wood, not stone, and the boards are fine, heavy old walnut planks as wide and tall as I am, and a number of them are still there, relatively undamaged. But I didn't want to be in that room any longer. I would burn every last piece of kitchen furniture before I went into that room again.

Adya must've understood. He didn't say a word about the floorboards. He sat at the kitchen table, rinsing his hands obediently in warm salt water in the cooking pot—he had rubbed the blisters raw under the wrappings—and watching while I closed up the cracks in the doorway. I took the sheet music, Chopin's waltz in C-sharp minor, from the drawer in the hutch and crumpled it up to fill in the gaps.

I don't know why I kept that music so long. The piano, my mother's 1832 Buchholtz piano of lovely yellow flamed maple wood that my father gave her as a wedding present, burned with the rest of the house. The sheet music survived the fire purely by accident. I found it strewn across the yard later. I kept it, I suppose, for the memory of happier days, as I kept Emi's letters. We danced that waltz in Vienna, he and I, at the Court Ball—our very first dance together.

But of course the music was quite worthless in itself, and truthfully I'd forgotten about it until Adya found it the day before. It served no practical purpose now; it might as well go toward shutting out the drafts. One becomes very pragmatic in wartime.

Adya, watching me crumple up the music and slip it into the cracks in the jambs, said, "You play?"

It was the first time either of us had said anything to the other beyond what was necessary or immediate—the first time either of us had said anything at all of life beyond this room, this house, this war. We were both, I think, hurting very much in that moment.

"Yes," I said, "a little"—with the sort of reflexive self-deprecation that women tend to append to our own accomplishments. I've played since I was four years old. I play very well.

He saw through it. Men do not always. "To hell with a little. You play Chopin."

The curious thing was that I'd copied out that music myself, by hand, from our old folio of Chopin's waltzes, which had been quite literally falling apart with age. I believe it was my mother's when she was young. I hadn't written out the composer or full title. I'd written only *cis-moll*, C-sharp minor, on the corner of the first page. It might've been anything in that key. If he recognized it as Chopin, he must be able to read music, and to hear it in his head as he did so.

There was very little else, I'd thought, that could surprise me about Adya. But that surprised me.

"Do you play?" I asked him.

"No."

"But you read music."

He shrugged. "My mother. She played. Her people had money." He flexed his fingers absently in the salt water. He seemed to recognize that this required further explanation, because suddenly he said, "She went slumming—married beneath her, whatever you want to call it. Had to make the best of it when he ran out on her; her people wouldn't lift a finger for her. The priest let her give lessons on the cathedral organ—that's how she kept food on the table. She tried to teach me. Waste of time, I never had a head for it. But I remember that waltz. She used to play that one. She tried to teach me to dance. She wanted to make something of me, you know? Something she could stand to look at. Something that didn't remind her of that piece of shit, my father."

"Perhaps," I said carefully, "perhaps she simply wished you to know that you needn't be like him. That you weren't fated to be like him. You were free to make something better of yourself."

He laughed that cold little breath of a laugh through his nostrils. "Well, it was a waste of time. I can't dance."

I said, "Why didn't you leave Vitya in the Lemberg camp?"

"What?"

"You knew he would slow you down. You knew he would cost you your chance at escape. Why didn't you leave him?"

"Why the hell do you think? He saved my life in Rovno."

"But you knew he wasn't likely to last more than a day out of the camp. You knew how developed the gangrene was—how quickly it was likely to spread. You knew there wasn't any point. He might as well have died in Lemberg as here. You gave up your own chance at freedom to bring him with you, and for what?"

"To hell with my own chance."

"I think that's the difference."

He laughed again. "So? My father could do you a good turn if you'd done him a good turn. He was still a bastard. It isn't some difference between us. Vitya did me a good turn. I did him a good turn."

"He trusted you," I said.

"No. He needed me. He needed his conscience cleared after Łąka, and I was his way to do it. And he owed me. I pushed him down a trench once in Dubno. Damn fool was walking around head and shoulders above the parapet. Nearly got his brains blown out."

I didn't press him further. He had been thickheaded with fever and with the warm haze of the krupnik earlier. He'd forgotten, I think, how I'd held him as he cried. Clearly, Vitya had been more to him than a debt to settle. But his defenses were up now, his heels dug in. Any kind word I might've offered him would've only added another plate to the armor he wore against his grief.

I tried a different tack. "It isn't difficult—the waltz step," I said.

"Hanon's excercises are easy if you play Chopin. Still pretty damn hard for the rest of us."

"Here—I'll show you," I said.

He looked up at me. Then he looked back at his hands in the salt water. Slowly, very slowly, he took his hands from the pot and dried them on my kitchen towel.

"Fucking waste of time," he said. But he scraped back his chair and got up.

We pushed the table and chairs up against the wall. We faced each other in the middle of the floor. It would've been difficult to dance with him in ordinary circumstances—the circumstances in which I, as a noblewoman, had been accustomed to dancing, in evening dress at formal balls or dinners. In heeled pumps, I would've been several centimeters taller than he, and it's always difficult when the leading partner is shorter. But we were about level in our boots.

My boots, like my coat, had been salvaged from the mortuary at the hospital. They had been some luckless Russian's. They were not very good boots. Rough brown felt without much sole to speak of, and though they were warm when dry, they were not waterproof. They were several sizes too big—ugly, shapeless things—but I had lined them with rags to make up the difference. I was long past worrying about being fashionable.

Adya stood motionless while I guided his hands into place: his left clasped in my right, his right pressed lightly to my back, between my shoulder blades. "There."

"It's all right?"

He wasn't asking, I think, about the technique of his positioning. But I pretended he was.

"Yes, that's good," I said. "And I put my hand on your shoulder, so . . ."

I slipped my hand over his right shoulder, and he exhaled very softly through his nostrils. I could feel him, tense and tight, under my palm.

"And now you step forward with your right foot, and I step back with my left . . ."

He stepped me back very carefully, watching my feet. His fingertips brushed lightly and uncertainly along my back. I could barely feel them through the thick wool of my coat. But still it was enough to bring back the memory of the last time I'd danced like this. Vienna, the grand ballroom at the Hofburg lit by dozens of sparkling crystal chandeliers, the swell of the violins from the Royal Orchestra in the wings, Emi's gloved hands on me.

Emi had been the one guiding me skillfully and patiently through that night. Not only through the dancing but through the dinner and the audience with the emperor and the endless introductions to barons and baronesses, counts and countesses, princes and princesses whose names and faces I've forgotten now. He, at twenty-two, was an old hand at both the Hofball, the Court Ball, and the even more exclusive Ball bei Hof two weeks later, whereas I at sixteen had never before been any farther from home than Lemberg, and it was all rather breathtaking.

How reassuring it had been to have him by my side—as if he were an old friend, as if we'd known each other for years, though we'd never laid eyes on each other before that night.

How very comforting, I had thought, to know that I would always have him by my side. How very lucky I was.

That was, of course, January of 1914, about six months before the war began.

"And now we turn," I said to Adya. "You bring your left foot around, like this . . ."

"Here?"

"Yes. And then your right."

We took a few turns around the perimeter of the kitchen. I showed him how to make the reverse turn, and we went back and forth between the natural and the reverse, slowly and carefully. He didn't speak except for those two brief questions.

He wasn't a bad dancer. Unpracticed and cautious, but not bad. The key to dancing is timing, and his sense of timing was very good. I suspected that more of his musical training had stuck than he admitted.

But it's meant to be a close dance, the waltz, intimate despite its pace—the Viennese waltz can be very fast—and he was reluctant to step very close, to slide his knee inside mine on the turns as one must do to execute them smoothly, to tighten his hands on me.

It wasn't just hesitation to touch me; his blistered hands were of course still hurting him badly.

He said all at once, still stepping me slowly around the floor, "You know I was giving you the chance to go."

"Last night?"

"Yes."

"Yes, I know."

"Why did you stay?"

And of course I couldn't explain myself to him then as thoroughly as I've explained myself to you now. I hadn't had four days in the solitude of a cell to sort through my scattered thoughts and feelings. The reasons were there in my head, but I hadn't yet practiced putting them into words.

I said only, "There was another boy once who died when I might've saved him. I suppose I wanted to balance the ledger."

"In the hospital?"

"In the village, last summer. A peasant boy. They hanged him as a collaborator—the Austrians."

"Another rusek." His voice was sour. "You have a history."

"Another boy whose death didn't solve anything."

He was silent for a moment, turning me carefully. I think he was finding it difficult to step the waltz and talk at the same time. Then he said, still sourly, "You never wanted vengeance? Death to the ruski?"

"That boy had done nothing to me. Vitya had done nothing to me."

"He was the enemy. This is war. Stop acting so fucking high-minded."

"That's a coward's excuse," I said softly. "I hope to God I'll always have a better answer for what I've done than 'this is war.'"

We had stopped dancing now, though he hadn't taken his hands from me. We had just finished a turn, and he hadn't stepped back this time. We were standing very close. I could hear the hitch in his breath.

He said, "No one will ever accuse you of being a coward, moja pani, I can promise you that."

Then he let me go, taking my hand from his shoulder. He was still running a fever, I think: His cheeks were flushed.

# CHAPTER 14

The irony is that quite a lot of people have accused me of being a coward in the six days since. A traitor and a collaborator and a whore too, but worst of all a coward.

It is not technically why I am on trial, and it is not what I will be sentenced for. There is no precedent, I think, for executing members of the imperial medical corps for cowardice, unlike soldiers of the line. But it is, perhaps, the deepest underlying root of the charges. If I were not a coward first, I would be none of these other things.

And it's the accusation that hits closest to home, that stings the most sharply.

But I suppose the very fact that I am still alive, alone of my family, bears witness against me. How could I betray their memory so completely as to aid and comfort the enemy who took them from me? How else, unless I am driven only by a weaseling sense of self-preservation?

My name and title mean very little now, and perhaps rightfully so. But I would much rather they mean nothing at all than that they become bywords for cowardice, as Kalikst

Witkowski's name became a byword for bloodthirst and lust for power. I would much rather my name be forgotten than still spat upon with loathing in the streets of Lemberg fifty years from now.

This is the thought that haunts me above all. This is the regret I'll carry to my grave. That you will not remember my father and brother, who died defiantly at the Russians' hands, or my mother, who chose with cold, terrible pride to end her own life rather than to live in subjection. That you will remember only Renata Krystyna Zamoyska, who broke her oath and disrupted the war effort. I owed them so much better than that.

Adya sat in the corner by the woodbin, his hands wrapped in fresh rags, and cut the window boards down with the bow saw while I made a soup with one of the dried brown trout. I boiled the fish in salt water until the flesh was soft; then I discarded the bones and tore up the flesh and returned it to the pot with two of the potatoes cut in pieces.

We sat at the table with the grease lamp between us and ate. A mimicry of ordinariness, as if just for this little while we could forget the war and the storm and the boy's body in the cellar below us and be two people sharing a meal in quiet lamplight.

Adya washed out my tin cup in the snow for me. He ate his soup from the pot lid turned upside down like a shallow bowl, balanced carefully in his wrapped hands. I have no spoons. We drank the broth and ate the bits of fish and potato with our fingers. It wasn't much of a soup, but it was hot and filling, and the salty vinegar taste of the fish was good, and there was enough left in the pot to keep for breakfast too. I've learned very well how to stretch one meal into two or three.

We hadn't spoken to each other since we danced. There had been no need. But Adya said to me all at once, without preamble, "Will you stay on at the hospital?"

It always catches me pleasantly by surprise when someone speaks of my work as if it's entirely unremarkable. I'm so used to explaining myself and defending myself. I've found that most wounded men don't much care who is treating them, but plenty of doctors regard it as an affront to work with a woman as an assistant. Doctor von Brenner is very magnanimous in this regard—his own daughter is a medical student at the University of Vienna—but there are others who will not work with me or who at least require Doctor von Brenner's assurances of my competence first.

"After the war, you mean," I said.

"Mm." Adya was bent over his bowl. His mouth was full.

"I'm not sure," I said. "Yes, I hope so. I'll need the work to pay my tuition. I was in pediatrics at the medical university."

Of course it's highly unlikely that they would've let me stay on in my present capacities. In peacetime, it's not standard procedure to let first-year students such as myself, whether men or women, perform the sorts of operations I've often performed out of necessity.

Adya swallowed his mouthful. He was eating as he'd eaten each time before—slowly, considering each bite unto itself, chewing very thoroughly before he swallowed.

"Pediatriya," he repeated. We were speaking Russian still. I believe he was most comfortable with Russian, or perhaps he used it as a shield of sorts. It's very nearly the same word in Russian and Polish—*pediatriya*, *pediatria*. I could tell he didn't know the word in any case.

"Children's medicine. I was specializing in children's surgery."

It was dangerous ground. I didn't want him thinking about the boy—didn't want him thinking that perhaps Vitya would've lived if only I had been the one to perform the amputation, didn't want him blaming himself for taking the knife from my hand. Vitya would've died just the same if I, or Doctor von Brenner for that matter, had been the one holding the blade.

"And you?" I asked him. "What about you? What will you do?"

"After the war?"

"Yes."

"Go home and wait for them to hang me, probably."

This was not just grief, but anger. I know the progression very well. I've seen it often enough in the hospital.

I said carefully, "When the word gets out about Łąka—about what you were ordered to do there—there may be enough of a public outcry that you'll be given a pardon. It's happened before."

"Four companies in my battalion. Four platoons in each company. Fifteen other platoon officers they had to choose from—fifteen other platoon officers they could've ordered to deal with Łąka, a Polish village. But they picked me, the only Polish officer in the whole battalion. I'd have to be an idiot to think it was an accident. There isn't going to be a pardon. I'm the scapegoat. As long as they've got insubordinate psheki like me to hang for defying orders, guess who's going to get the blame for losing Lemberg—for losing Łuck—for losing the whole fucking Privislinsky Krai? Fucking treacherous little psheki, that's who. There isn't going to be a pardon."

"Things may be different after the war," I said.

"Not for people like me."

I knew he thought I didn't understand. To show him that I did, or at least that I wanted to, I said, "Where is home?"

He was working his way methodically around the makeshift bowl, eating the lumps of fish and potato one by one, catching the drippings with his thumb.

"Lublin," he said. "Pawia Street, near the railyard. I made three rubles a week shifting freight." He was silent for a moment, chewing. "Made better money stealing guns from the yard and selling them to the anarchists. There was a chapter of Rewolucyjni Mściciele in Lublin."

It struck me that he really must believe his only possible future was to hang. I doubt he would've made such a confession otherwise. At least, I doubt he would've made it to me. He knew I was szlachcianka. I don't suppose that anyone would admit to a noblewoman one's involvement with a terrorist organization such as Rewolucyjni Mściciele, which has no qualms about the use of violence against both the bourgeoisie and the landed class, unless one was either reckless or utterly hopeless. And Lieutenant Kijek did not strike me as reckless.

"Are you an anarchist?"

"I was hungry."

After a pause, I ventured, "I've been to Lublin."

"Not anywhere near Pawia Street you haven't."

He was right, of course. I've been just that once to Russian Poland. My mother and I and Countess Potocka took the train to Warsaw to see Rubinstein perform Chopin at the Warsaw Philharmonic, and we spent a night in Lublin en route, as Lublin is almost exactly halfway between Lemberg and Warsaw. I was sixteen and officially "out" in society, having made my appearance at court. It was the spring of 1914, that spring after I danced in

Emi's arms at the Court Ball in January. We stayed at the Hotel Victoria, quite grand and glittering, and took champagne cocktails at one of the clubs on Krakowskie Przedmieście, I couldn't tell you which, followed by an eight-course dinner *à la russe* at the Belvedere.

I knew enough of the world and of my place in it to be conscious of the excess even then. But there was a peculiarly acute sense of shame in thinking of these things now, with Adya there at my kitchen table—knowing that he might've been down at the Lublin railyard that very same spring night two years ago, selling stolen weapons to Rewolucyjni Mściciele for grocery money, while I dined on oysters and quail and drank Romanée-Conti at the Belvedere.

He tipped the lid to drain the last bit of broth—not a drop going to waste.

"Maybe things will be different," he said. "Maybe after the war we'll grovel to the kaiser instead of the tsar."

Of course these were Lieutenant Kijek's words, not mine. And we were both hurting just then, as I've said, so we were prone to speaking emotionally. I am aware that it does not help my case before a German court to imply, in any way, that the kaiser is on a level with the tsar or that the status of being a German subject is akin to groveling.

I covered the pot of soup to keep until morning. I boiled a bit of snow in my tin cup and went behind our little privacy curtain to wash my face and to comb and rebraid my hair.

It was very quaint of me, I suppose, to let my hair down behind the curtain so that Adya wouldn't see. The tradition is that a girl wears her hair braided until her wedding night, that only a loose girl lets her hair down in public, but of course one isn't thinking of that in wartime. I wear the braid not for modesty but because it's hygienic and practical in the operating theater. It was foolish, in our present circumstances, to suppose it made much difference whether Adya saw me with my hair undone.

He was still at the table when I came out from behind the curtain. He was cleaning his pistol with a bit of rag in the glow of the grease lamp, stripping it apart piece by piece on the tabletop, his fingers swift and deft despite the blisters. He worked with the same precision and skill with which he'd prepared the birch boughs the day before. He snapped the slide to eject the chambered round; he took out the magazine and dispensed the spare rounds into his palm. He set the snub-nosed little cartridges up in a neat row on the tabletop, like dominoes.

There were five of them. A Mauser pistol such as his, the 1914 model, has an eight-round magazine. I know this because my father kept one of the same model—that was, in fact, the pistol that my mother used to end her life. This pistol of Adya's had been used at some point.

"I'll watch the fire," I said to him.

He held the empty pistol in his left hand and removed the pin, then the barrel, then the slide, setting each on the tabletop in turn. "I'm watching it. Go to sleep."

I wasn't afraid of that pistol, even knowing he had very likely used it to kill. He could've used it on me long before if he'd wanted to. But I was very much afraid to leave him there alone in the dark and the silence with the pistol, and his anger, and his grief, and his guilt, and his hopelessness.

I swept the rounds, all five of them, off the tabletop and into my hand.

"Give me your knife," I said.

He was silent, holding the shell of the pistol in his hand,

looking across the room at nothing. Then he reached with his free hand and took his pocketknife from somewhere inside his coat. He laid it in my hand. He didn't look at me.

I put the cartridges and the knife in the waist pocket of my coat. "Wake me up when you need to," I said.

I didn't sleep right away. I lay awake in my corner for a long time, bundled in my coat, watching him work in the soft flickering half-light.

I suppose for a while I was worried that he might try to take his cartridges back once he thought I was asleep, and I had some idea that I might stop him as long as I was awake. But I wasn't really afraid of him, any more than I'd been afraid of that pistol. Anything he might've done to me, he would've done already.

But I had grown so used to being alone. There had been no one else with me in that house since June. I'd grown used to the stillness and the silence. It was unsettling to know he was there—to close my eyes and still sense him there in the dark. To open my eyes again and see him in his Russian uniform. I hadn't had time to think about it the previous night. I'd been too utterly exhausted. But I lay awake thinking about it now.

I fell asleep finally. He was still there at the table, silhouetted against the glow of the grease lamp, leaning on his elbows on the tabletop, picking up each piece of the pistol and turning it in his hand and wiping it with the rag, piece after piece after piece, like a loop of a motion picture . . .

And then the loop slipped off the spool, and he got up from the table and unbuttoned his coat and brought it over and draped it gently over me, being very careful not to touch me, and I knew this part must be a dream, and I didn't move because I didn't want it to end just yet.

I was back in Vienna. It was January of 1914, the night of the Court Ball, after midnight. We had just left the Hofburg and were driving back in Emi's chauffeured limousine through the sleeping Innere Stadt, back along the Ringstrasse to the Palais Schönborn-Batthyány. The car went very slowly and carefully because snow had started to fall, spinning over the cobblestones and gathering like a burial shroud on the statue of Empress Elisabeth in the Volksgarten.

Emi and I were alone in the back of the car, and I had only my flimsy evening coat of silk and sheer lace. Emi unbuttoned his officer's greatcoat of soft, heavy gray wool and draped it around my shoulders and pulled it close, and then very swiftly he bent his dark head and kissed me—the first and only time a boy has ever kissed me.

And I stayed very still, my eyes tightly shut, because I thought maybe if I didn't move or speak or open my eyes I wouldn't lose him. If I could stay just as I was in this moment, I wouldn't lose him.

But of course it's less than two kilometers from the Hofburg to the Palais, and the drive does not take very long even in the snow.

I woke up much later in bitter, bitter cold.

It was long past midnight—I knew instinctively that I had slept for a long time. Adya was on his knees in front of the stove. He had the grille thrown open, and he was lighting a twist of scrap paper with the little sputtering flame of the grease lamp.

"What's wrong?"

"Downdraft," he said. "The fire's out. And I think something's blocking the pipe. I can't relight it."

I was awake all at once. One wakes very quickly in such sharp cold. It had not been entirely a dream. Adya's coat fell away when I stood.

# CHAPTER 15

I am telling you all this because I might as well clear up a misunderstanding.

I have no argument with the charges as formalized by Captain Baran and corroborated by Corporal Pawlik. I think I've made that very clear from the beginning. I will be sentenced, I'm told, for "actions deemed disruptive to the war effort" because I attempted to prostitute myself to an imperial officer.

I agree that offering myself to Captain Baran because I wanted something from him in return fits the definition of prostitution, which remains officially illegal within the empire unless one has registered with the authorities and undergone the requisite monthly medical examinations.

And I agree on principle that prostituting myself to an imperial officer could be considered disruptive to the war effort and should not be encouraged.

Nor do I wish to be uncharitable or ungrateful. I should be clear about that too. I believe that in all of this Captain Baran acted primarily out of concern for my well-being or at least for my honor, as he saw it.

But he has accused me of sleeping with Lieutenant Kijek, and the only evidence he has presented for this claim is that on the morning of January third, when he and his men finally dug their way through the snow to my door, he found us in close proximity; and that when he put a pistol against the lieutenant's head, I asked him—in accordance with the laws of war regarding the treatment of prisoners—to spare the lieutenant's life.

I suppose it's rather foolish of me to worry about a detail like this when I've freely confessed to prostituting myself. But all the same, I wish to clarify this point, for the lieutenant's sake as much as my own.

You needn't believe me. I am fully aware that it does not absolve me of guilt or indeed have much bearing at all, since I am not technically on trial for sleeping with Lieutenant Kijek any more than I am technically on trial for cowardice.

But I did not sleep with Lieutenant Kijek out of moral weakness or lust, and he certainly did not force me.

I slept with him—in the sense that he was asleep and I was asleep and we were next to each other—because it was twelve degrees centigrade below zero and the stove had gone out.

The likeliest explanation, I thought, was that an iced-over tree limb had snapped in that sudden draft of wind and fallen across the roof, obstructing the stovepipe. The sound would of course have been muffled by the depth of accumulated snow. There are those larch trees quite close along the southern side of the house, as I've said, and I was already well aware of the dangers they posed.

I told Adya this, and he started to put his coat back on, but I said, "I'll go."

I didn't want him out in that cold for any length of time with his frostbitten hands, and I knew what I was doing. It's possible to reach the roof from the kitchen stoop, as the eave hangs low. What had been the upper story of the house—the later addition, the part that burned in June—used to overhang the kitchen, and one could drop from the upper-story window onto the kitchen roof and thence into the yard. Mieszko, always much brasher than I, used it as a convenient way to slip unnoticed in and out of the house when he was a boy, and he showed me how to do it. I've never been a rule-breaker—at least, I've never thought of myself as one, though I suppose the fact that I am standing before this tribunal belies me a little—and I was never brave enough to try it myself, but I was very proud to be his confidante and never betrayed him.

I put Adya's coat over my coat. I wore his cap instead of mine because his was the Cossack-style papakha, the kind with fur-lined ear flaps that may be folded up or down, and it was big enough to pull down quite low over my brow. With my scarf knotted around my mouth and nose and his scarf around my neck, there was very little of my face left exposed.

My gloves were not ideal. I knitted them myself, as I've not had the money to buy good fur-lined ones, and I am an unpracticed needlewoman. My mother and grandmother both labored to teach me, as it is a prized art for a Polish woman, and I'm sorry to say that their efforts were in vain. I have no skill for needlework beyond suturing flesh, it seems. The knit of those gloves is quite loose in places. But they were far better protection than those bits of thin rag on Adya's hands.

I took the coal bucket and set to work digging my way out from the kitchen door onto the stoop, using the lip of the bucket as a sort of shovel. I moved about by feel and by memory; I could see very little. It was pitch dark in the yard. It was five or six o'clock in the morning and still snowing fiercely, and of course I'd shut the door behind me to save as much heat as possible, which meant I didn't have the light from the grease lamp.

The wind, howling down slantwise across the yard, was sharp enough to draw tears, which went almost immediately to ice on my eyelashes.

It must've taken me half an hour just to dig myself out enough that I could find the low overhanging eave of the roof above me. By then my fingers were stiff nearly to the point of immobility, burning with the cold.

But I turned the coal bucket upside down on the edge of the stoop and, with the bow saw slung over my shoulder, pulled myself up onto the eave using the bucket as a step, trying to upset as little of the snow on the roof as possible. I would have better traction on the soft, fresh-fallen snow than on the ice-slick ceramic tiles beneath.

I didn't try to stand up in that cutting wind. I worked my way slowly on my hands and knees up the slope of the roof toward the ridge.

I came across the fallen limb about halfway up the slope. It was a long, heavy old larch limb, crusted thickly with ice—far too heavy for me simply to shift it off, though I wasted some time trying. It had fallen in such a way that it blocked my path to the ridge of the roof. The stovepipe came up on the far slope past the ridge, so I would have to get past it one way or another.

I thought I would at least have a try at cutting my way through it before I made Adya come up and help me. I was thinking of his frostbitten hands, of course, but I don't deny that there was also an element of pride. It's difficult for anyone to admit defeat, but particularly difficult for a woman, because she knows very well how it may be used against her afterward, no matter how often and in how many other ways she has proved herself.

In any case, I did not ask Adya to come up. I balanced carefully on my knees there on the slope and took the bow saw from my shoulder.

I remember the sudden sick lurch in my stomach as my knees slipped. I remember nothing else until Adya's voice broke into my head all at once: "Moja pani."

I was lying flat on my back in a deep cushion of snow. I had fallen from the roof and landed in the drift below the eave. I had lain there for a good long while, I think—long enough that I was no longer cold, which is a dangerous thing. It was very difficult to make myself move.

I had hit the hard stone edge of the stoop when I fell. I was not disoriented or confused; I knew exactly where I was and how I'd come to be there. But the impact had knocked me unconscious, and there was a dull ache in my head and a long, sharp pain running under my right arm each time I drew a breath, and I did not want to move.

"Moja pani," Adya repeated. He was kneeling beside me in the snow, bending close, though he didn't touch me. I couldn't see him in the dark, but I could feel the warm gust of his breath on my cheek. "Moja pani, get up."

It occurred to me that I had dropped the saw when I fell.

It was this, more than anything else, that made me move finally. We wouldn't be able to find the saw once the snow covered it, certainly not in the dark, and if we couldn't shift that limb then we would have to cut through it, and for that we would need the saw.

"The saw," I said to Adya. I was lightheaded with the pain. "I dropped the saw."

"To hell with the saw."

"We need to find it, or we won't be able to open the stovepipe."

He said something under his breath. Then he said, "I'll find it. Go inside. Take those boots off and dry them."

Inside, I sat down on the hearth before the dead stove. I shed my scarf and gloves and his coat, moving very slowly. I couldn't get my boots off. I couldn't bend to tug at the heels. The pain under my arm was very sharp, and my head was swimming.

Adya came in, kicking out the tramped-in snow and shutting the door.

"Did you find it?" I asked him.

"Yes, I found it. It's outside the door. Why the hell haven't you taken your boots off? Put them under the firebox—get them dry while you can. Your stockings too. Do you want fucking trench foot?"

I didn't answer. I didn't want to tell him that I'd broken a rib through my own stupidity—bruised, at least, but I was fairly certain it was broken—and I didn't trust myself to speak without my voice shaking.

I unwound his scarf from my neck. There was blood on my hands when I pulled the scarf away. I must've cut my head when I fell—I must've landed on my side along the edge of the stoop and hit my head behind my right ear.

I wasn't quick enough to hide the blood from Adya. He came over from the doorway. He was, of course, wearing only his uniform and boots and those strips of rag about his hands; I had taken his coat and hat and scarf. I'd been too dazed to remember. I shouldn't have let him stay outside looking for that saw.

He knelt beside me. "Let me see the wound."

"It's nothing. Head wounds bleed."

"A split skull fucking bleeds."

I took off his hat and moved my braid aside for him, parting the roots of my hair with my fingers. There was a sore, swollen knot just above the rim of my ear. He spent a moment looking it over in the half-light. He leaned close; I could feel the warmth of his breath on my neck. But he did not touch me.

"I'll make a compress," he said.

He brought me a clump of packed snow folded in a dish towel, and I held it to the knot above my ear. The room was spinning. I wanted very much to lie down but didn't trust myself to do so without groaning or flinching. I didn't want Adya to know how badly I was hurting. I was ashamed for him to know. He had, after all, kept those horrid lacerations on his arm from me for the better part of a day. And there were more pressing concerns at hand.

He lingered beside me, crouched on his heels. "Moja pani," he said, "if you can't take off your boots, I'll need to do it."

"Yes," I said calmly, "yes, I think you'll have to."

He took off my sodden boots as he had taken off Vitya's, holding my heel gently in his hand as he slid the boot from my foot. He folded down the soft felt uppers and pulled out the damp wads of rags that I'd used to line the soles. He pushed the boots up under the ashpit beneath the stove. Then he reached for my knee stockings.

They were ugly things, knitted of plain, stout gray wool, practical rather than fashionable, and I can't imagine that Adya, under any circumstances, would've found them titillating. They were cold and wet, and they needed to be dried while there was still some heat left in the ashpit. I don't think he gave it any more thought than that. But I flinched when his hands went under my skirt, and he recoiled at once as if he'd been stung.

"Moja pani—"

"It's all right."

"We need to take them off."

"Yes," I said. "Yes, it's all right. Please take them off."

He took them off. He undid the garter straps and pulled the stockings down from my knees one after the other. He laid the stockings alongside my boots beneath the ashpit. There was nothing more to it. We might've been comrades at an aid station on the line.

He got up afterward and pulled on his coat and hat and went out, tying his scarf about his face as he went.

We had lost more than an hour on my account. The limb had lain there beneath a deepening mantle of snow all this time and would be harder to shift now. I've had time over the past four days to consider how very differently things might've turned out if not for my own foolish pride that morning.

I took the opportunity, when he had gone out, to unbutton my coat, tugging the front of my apron aside and opening my blouse and camisole and corset to feel out my rib cage. One rib was certainly broken. I could feel the break under my fingers through the thin muslin of my chemise.

I fastened everything back up and lay down very carefully on the hearth with my coat drawn over me like a blanket, Adya's compress against my ribs. I fell asleep, though I didn't mean to.

I woke when I heard Adya kicking snow from his boots in the doorway. I sat up quickly. I shouldn't have let myself fall asleep.

"Did you open the stovepipe?"

He swept the snow out and shut the door. "No," he said. He unwrapped the strips of wet rag from his hands. And then, shortly: "I lied to you earlier. Didn't find the saw. I was just trying to shift the thing off. Couldn't move it a fucking centimeter."

He came over and spent a moment warming his hands over the feeble little flame of the grease lamp on the stovetop. His fingers were choked red, the color of ripe sumac. Then he took another handful of scraps from my rag bag and started methodically to wrap up his hands again.

I said to him, "What are you doing?"

"Going to find the saw."

"You'll lose your hands if the frostbite gets any worse."

"If we can't relight the stove," he said, "you and I will be dead by tomorrow."

He was gone for a long time. I pulled on my stockings and rag-lined boots again. They were still damp but no longer dripping. I fell back asleep despite myself and woke in utter darkness.

The grease lamp on the stovetop was out, the wick having burned low and drowned. It didn't matter now whether we dislodged the fallen limb; without the lamp, we had no way to relight the stove. The embers in the ashpit were cold. I was clearheaded enough to check.

I heard Adya moving about in the dark, stamping the snow from his boots and sweeping it out the door.

"The lamp went out," I told him. I wasn't clearheaded enough to realize that of course he could see this for himself.

He shut the door. He said, "Who's the nearest neighbor?"

"The Kaplans. A kilometer to the north, across open fields. We won't make it in the snow."

"I didn't mean *we*. You know the ground. Take my coat. It's a better chance than you've got here."

I said, "Our best chance is to stay sheltered and dry. They'll send help from the village when the snow stops."

It was not a lie in the strictest sense, but it was not the whole truth.

Help wouldn't come right away. Berek Kaplan, at fourteen, is the oldest boy left in Zarudce, and he had of course been sick in bed since Wednesday. Father Urban is the only man of military age—he was in fact called up as a chaplain when the war started but was sent home on account of his rheumatism. These two and Pani Maslak, our schoolteacher, are the ones who help me organize relief efforts in the village when we have emergencies of this sort, and the resources at our disposal are very few.

We have no horses left since the occupation. The Russians, in preparation for their offensive against Przemyśl, commandeered every horse in the village within the first month, from the oldest swaybacked draft horse to the Lipizzan mare Emi gifted me for my sixteenth birthday. I'd written to him that I hoped at some point to see the haute école performed at the Spanish riding school in Vienna, and he went down to Lipica himself and chose her for me from the stud farm there and sent her to me in a heated boxcar. It hurt very much to lose her—worse to imagine that Emi might've spotted her from the walls of Przemyśl, toting some Russian officer about. Unlikely, I know, but I can't help thinking about it.

The Russians took most of our other stock during the retreat, took them or shot them, which means that the farmers of Zarudce will be in a hard way come plowing time this spring.

All this to say, it might've taken hours for help to reach us on foot from the village once the snow stopped, and it might easily have taken days. If help *were* to come right away—and this was the part I should've told the lieutenant but didn't—it might very well come from Lemberg, from the garrison, and he might very well go right back to the holding camp he'd made such an effort to escape.

I said none of this to him because I was very sure just then that if I left him there in that kitchen while I tried for the Kaplans' on my own, he would not be alive when I returned. I did not want to leave him alone.

And anyway I didn't consider it all that likely that anyone would come from the garrison, and I didn't want to worry him needlessly. Truth be told, I underestimated Captain Baran.

# CHAPTER 16

I've spent more than a year now wondering whether I might've done more to prevent my mother's suicide.

We received the telegram informing us of my father's death in December of 1914, just before Christmas, not from the Russian ministry of war but from young Jerzy Kalinowski, who had been my father's adjutant and who'd been with him on the failed mission to rescue my brother. He'd then gone with him into captivity at the camp at Sretensk, not very far from the northern borders of China—more than seven thousand kilometers from Lemberg.

The sheer scale of the distance is shocking to me even now. And it worries me. To think of all our prisoners there, swallowed up in the vastness of Siberia, so far from home. To think how many of them will never make it back—not because of sickness or mistreatment in the camp but simply because the steppe is so unthinkably large and home so impossibly far. How easy it must be for a person to slip silently through the cracks in seven thousand kilometers of wilderness.

I had a longer letter from Captain Kalinowski some months later, in April, explaining the circumstances of my father's death in more detail. There had been a typhus epidemic in the camp. In the absence of any trained medical staff in that remote place apart from the prisoners' own medics, my father, who was I think the ranking officer in the camp at that time, had taken it upon himself to organize efforts to contain the epidemic, putting himself at great risk of exposure.

But of course all we had at first was one line in a telegram: *REGRET TO INFORM YOU HIS EXCELLENCY COUNT ZAMOYSKI DEAD OF TYPHUS FEVER.*

My mother was not outwardly distraught in the days that followed the arrival of Captain Kalinowski's telegram. She was perhaps rather more aloof than usual—silent and listless. But then, we all were. In those first few days, we were all moving about by rote, unable to eat or sleep or take interest in anything. I would recognize it now as a form of shell shock, as I've seen it often enough in the hospital, even in patients who have no physical wounds and who seem perfectly healthy to observers.

But I didn't know enough then to recognize it for what it was—for how dangerous it was. I was mostly worried about Mieszko, to be honest.

I knew he blamed himself that my father had ended up a prisoner in the first place, and he was the hot-blooded one. Of the three of us, I thought he was the one most likely to do something rash. There was a Russian officer billeted with us at the time—partly from necessity, I think, and partly as Mieszko's jailer—and I was very careful to make sure that the two of them were never alone. He was a tall, thin boy, that Russian, lean as a garden stake, and even convalescent as he was, Mieszko could've snapped his neck with one hand.

I suppose that was my mistake, wasn't it? I was looking only for something hot-blooded and rash. The despair of a Puccini heroine, Tosca keening over her dead lover's body and flinging herself from the castle parapet.

My mother did not weep, or rage, or curse the Russians, or curse God. She did not cry out for justice or swear vengeance. She would not, I think, have flung herself from a castle parapet. But she could, quietly, in perfect calmness and without drawing any attention to herself, take my father's pistol up alone into her apple orchard.

I told Adya that we ought to eat while we could, before the food froze. He brought over the jar of pickled herring so we could share it between us. I managed one bite of that fish and knew I could eat no more. The pain under my arm was making my stomach jump. I didn't want to waste any of that fish by being sick.

I thought Adya wouldn't notice in the dark, but he did and misunderstood. Without a word, he got up again and brought my tin cup over from the table for me so I wouldn't have to dip my fingers into the jar with his.

I said, "No—my head just hurts a little."

I didn't want to admit the hurt to him. But it would've been worse to let him think I would not deign to share a common dish with him.

"Lie down," he commanded. "Keep still. I'll bring you another compress."

He brought another handful of snow knotted in his scarf, and I lay down gratefully on the hearth with the scarf bundled under my head like a soft, cool pillow. I was hurting very badly. I shut my eyes and listened to the throb of blood in my ears.

I drifted to sleep and woke up quite some time later,

thickheaded and lightheaded at once—the feeling one has when one comes back up to the surface after a long time underwater or when one wakes up sweating after a fever breaks.

It was a little lighter in the kitchen. Dull gray daylight was seeping in through the cracks in the doorjambs and the little gaps in the window bricking. It was very cold. My bare face burned and stung. The snow in the compress had melted under my head and run out and then turned to ice in my hair.

Adya sat beside me in nothing but his uniform, his head leant back against the wall, his hands at his sides, his eyes blank and distant. His breath made little wisps of silver cloud on the frozen air. His coat lay over me, soft and warm and heavy. He had done his best to get his hat onto my head without touching me. It was perched carefully on my forehead rather like a stork's nest balanced on the ridge of a barn roof. It slipped off when I turned my face to him.

He was waiting to die. He had been resolved to die, I think, since he offered me his coat and told me to go alone to the Kaplans'. I missed the signs in my mother; I will never miss them again.

"What time is it?" I asked him.

"Two o'clock," he said to the far wall, "a little after."

"Has the snow stopped?"

"Not yet. Go back to sleep."

"You need your coat."

"You need to rest your head. Go back to sleep," he repeated.

"Get under the coat," I said to him.

He looked at me. Then he looked quickly away. A muscle fluttered in his cheek.

"Moja pani—" he started, his voice low.

"Get under the coat, Adya," I said to him very gently.

You may debate, if you wish, whether the sin was mine for telling him to do it or his for doing it; I don't know. I know that if I hadn't told him to do it, and if he hadn't done it, he would've been one more boy needlessly dead when I might've saved him.

And yet I held my breath while he lifted the coat and lay down beside me. There was no hint of a threat in his closeness. He didn't reach for me or angle his body toward me. He didn't even look at me. But my hands shook as I smoothed out the coat and spread it over both of us.

It's always in my mind now. It's where my thoughts go first when a man tips his hat to me on the street or when a boy smiles at me from his hospital bed. What might he do to me, this boy, if he wanted to—if there were no constraints upon him but his own conscience? What might he have done if he had been here that day in June? If Adya wanted to, he could overpower me very easily. I could only trust that he did not want to.

We lay side by side under the coat. He was shuddering violently, his whole body trembling with spasms that seemed to roll over him in waves. I don't know how long he'd been sitting there without his coat, but it might very well have been five hours or more; I had been asleep, I think, since about seven o'clock. I said softly, "You should've woken me."

"You need to sleep. I know about head wounds."

"We lose body heat when we sleep. We both need to stay awake."

"When the snow stops," he said, "you should try for the neighbor's."

"I can't."

"I'll be here if they come here first. I'll tell them where to look for you. But you know the ground, and it's fucking stupid for both of us to lie here freezing—"

"I can't," I said. "I broke a rib when I fell. I don't think I can walk a kilometer."

I didn't want to tell him. But I had seen that stillness in him, that emptiness in his eyes, and I knew how very close I was to losing him. I knew I wouldn't lose him just yet if he believed he was needed still. We've found in the hospital that in such cases it is often helpful to give the patients particular tasks or responsibilities that they may make their own.

He said, "That's it. I'm going."

"No."

"You need a doctor."

"I am a doctor. It's all right. It's manageable. But if you show up on the Kaplans' doorstep, they'll turn you in, do you understand? They'll do it because they have to. They'll do it because if the word gets out that they sheltered a Russian officer, they'll hang."

He was silent. Then he said, "And you? When the word gets out?"

"I am Countess Zamoyska," I said. "They won't hang me."

As it turns out, this was not entirely a lie. I didn't know then that I would be tried before a military tribunal. You will of course shoot me, not hang me.

# CHAPTER 17

I don't know how much experience you all have with hypothermia and exposure. I have a good deal.

We treat it fairly often in the hospital, though less often now that the fighting has moved so far east and we're no longer dealing as much in first aid. But I can tell that many of our doctors have never dealt with it before, beyond hypotheticals in a university classroom. Doctor von Brenner is one of the few. He worked with the Foundlings' Home in Vienna before the war, and he tells me that very often those children—abandoned or orphaned and living on the street—came to the home suffering from hypothermia to varying degrees. But many of our other doctors, the younger ones and the wealthier ones especially, had never seen an actual case until the war.

I had. There was never any electricity in the Zarudce house, no gas, no running water. The great room was heated with the type of tiled masonry stove that has been used for centuries in this part of the world. That iron cookstove in the kitchen is one of the only concessions my father allowed to modernity, and it is woodfired even so.

So we felt our winters very keenly. I learned to look for and recognize the signs of hypothermia long before I knew the scientific name. We called it snow sleep because, as the body begins to succumb to the cold, the brain slowly loses function and the victim feels overcome with exhaustion. In the most severe stages, the victim is physically unable to stay awake.

I mention this because I do not believe that Captain Baran, when he found us on the morning of the third, understood how very serious the lieutenant's condition was. I think this may have contributed to the misunderstandings that followed.

I do not believe that Captain Baran had ever before seen a man nearly dead of cold. I do not believe he has ever experienced hypothermia himself, nor do I believe he has any idea of the symptoms or of how to treat them. He is not szlachta but comes from money all the same, his father having made his fortune in railroads, I believe. He is a divisional staff officer. He has never lived under occupation, and he has never himself set foot near the front.

**Captain Baran says, "You—you, Countess—are suggesting that I am a coward?"**

**His face is white with fury, but his voice is carefully calm. This is the first time he has dared speak since Colonel Sosnkowski's warning. It is the first time he has spoken to me directly since the arrest.**

**"I am suggesting that perhaps you misread the situation because you did not know—"**

**"I know what hypothermia is, Countess. I know the symptoms."**

**"With respect, Captain, I don't believe you understood the severity of the lieutenant's case. It was necessary to raise his body temperature to keep him alive."**

"Necessary, Countess? He is the enemy. There was nothing necessary about keeping him alive."

"I have been explaining why I found it necessary."

"You needn't bother. We all know the truth."

"Baran"—another warning from Colonel Sosnkowski.

"Deny it, Countess. We all know you were fucking him."

"Captain Baran, you're dismissed."

"You've spun this whole story because you're too proud to admit you spent three days fucking a Muscovite guttersnipe so he wouldn't put a bullet in your head, like a dirty little Scheherazade."

"Sergeant"—Colonel Sosnkowski, addressing the officer of the Militärpolizei at the doors—"remove Captain Baran from the courtroom."

"No—if you please, Colonel," I say. "I would like the opportunity to explain myself in Captain Baran's hearing. He is my accuser; I would like to answer him directly."

Captain Baran says, "Yes, answer me, Countess, and remember that you believe in the sacredness of giving your word. Nine months after the Graf von Schönborn's death, and 'ukochana Renia' has taken up with an unlettered anarchist gunrunner from the Lublin railyards."

A stretch of dead silence, broken by a sudden scuffling at the back of the room. Lieutenant Kijek, attempting to lunge to his feet and being sat back down rather forcibly by his guards on either side. I'm not sure whether he has understood the insult to himself, but he may well have understood the reference to Emi's letters.

"My apologies, Colonel Sosnkowski," I say very calmly. "On second thought, yes: I would like Captain Baran removed from the room."

I don't remember much of that last afternoon, the afternoon of January second. It has all run together in my head. Adya couldn't stop shuddering. It was too cold, even beside me under the coat, for him to make up the body heat he had lost. It was increasingly difficult to keep him awake. I would feel him drift off—I would feel his muscles loosen. He would start awake again when I said his name, shoulders jerking. Then he would swear under his breath and settle back down again beside me. A little while later, he would drift off again.

But I do remember his saying unexpectedly, "Who is Emi?"

It caught me off guard. Not because it was so sudden—I understood by now that he had little use or patience for small talk—but because I'd forgotten that he had come across those letters in the hutch when he made his search of the kitchen that first night. It took me a moment to remember where he might've seen the name.

I said, "Did you read them?"

"No. I saw the names. I saw the greeting."

*Renia, ukochana moja*—Renia, my beloved. They were not necessarily love letters on the evidence of that greeting alone. *Ukochana* is a tender word in Polish but not, of course, an inherently romantic one. They might've been letters from a relative or a close family friend. The young Graf von Schönborn-Buchheim never signed his personal letters to me with his full title, only with "Emi" or "Your Emi."

I admit I pondered for a moment whether I should tell Adya that the letters were from a cousin. If he hadn't read them, he would know no better.

But I said, "He was my fiancé. Emil. He was killed at Przemyśl during the siege."

You all know better than I, I'm sure, the details of the siege of the great fortress at Przemyśl, ninety kilometers west of here, and its aftermath. Lemberg had of course already fallen by then; we were under Russian occupation at the time and heard very little reliable news from the front as it moved westward. We knew that the fortress had finally fallen in March, with the loss of nearly a hundred and forty thousand men killed or captured, but I didn't learn of Emi's death until July, nearly a month after liberation.

Adya was silent beside me. I thought he must've drifted to sleep again. But then he said, "I'm sorry."

And I, having been brought up to spurn pity—or, at least, to never make a show of my own grief in order to invite pity—said by reflex, "It was an arranged match."

This was not a lie. The arrangement had been contracted by my father and the elder Graf von Schönborn-Buchheim when I was fourteen and Emi twenty, two years before we met for the first time. But one could be forgiven for thinking I meant that the match was purely political. If Adya had thought so, I wouldn't have corrected him.

But he, far too sharp to be misled, said, "You kept his letters."

"Yes."

"You loved him?"

It seems so long ago now, so distant, like a half-remembered dream. I had come to know and love Emi through his letters before I ever laid eyes on him. He had been the one to initiate correspondence, and the start was not auspicious. His first letter had come, of course, from Vienna, from the garrison barracks, stamped with the imperial eagle, and I, foolishly, thought it was from Mieszko, who was then at the war college and whom I missed terribly. Imagine my disappointment at opening that letter and finding that it was instead from a complete stranger—identifying himself as my future husband, no less. In an accident of timing, or in a remarkable demonstration of the efficiency of the imperial postal service, Emi's letter reached me before my father had concluded his business trip and made it back from Vienna to bring me the news himself.

Emi had written in German and enclosed a photograph of himself. He must've known how dashing a figure he cut, tall and dark and debonair in his cavalry officer's uniform. I had, rather coldly, written him back in Polish—a small act of pride and defiance. I was sure he thought of me as uncultured and rustic, and I didn't mind letting him underestimate me, as that could give me something of an advantage later. But he had replied in Polish without missing a beat, and from then on I was his.

There was an element of hero-worship in the way I felt about him; I was of course very young. He was six years older, already an officer of the Vienna garrison, with a quick wit and a keen, serious mind. And yet he never spoke down to me or treated me as anything other than his equal.

From what I saw of him in Vienna, this was the manner in which he treated everyone, regardless of sex or standing. It made quite an impression on me that he knew the given names of each footman and staff member at the Hotel Bristol and the Café Central and the Schwarzenberg, down to the cloakroom attendant. My only other experience with a suitor had been with the young Count Potocki, who'd been far more interested in my father's racehorses than in me and certainly couldn't have told you the names of any of the stable hands.

"Yes," I said to Adya, "I loved him."

"You met him?"

"Only once. Two years ago, at the Court Ball in Vienna. But we had corresponded before that."

Adya let out that little breath of a laugh. "The Court Ball in Vienna."

"It's a rule of etiquette. A young woman of noble rank must be presented at court before she may come out in society. I was presented at the ball that January."

"Fucking cattle market. Hawking you off like a Polish Red heifer."

"Yes, there are similarities." It was not the case for me, as I was already affianced, but it's no secret that the Vienna ball season serves as a sort of bride-show among the empire's elite families.

"What the hell was he doing in Przemyśl? If he was going to court balls in Vienna, he wasn't posted to a backwater like Przemyśl."

"No. He was a cavalry officer of the Vienna garrison. He requested a transfer to the Third Army here in Galicia when the war began. He was with the relief force that broke through the siege lines in October. He was wounded then. He remained in the city with the garrison when the rest of the Third retreated. He had hoped to make his way eventually here to Lemberg."

"For you?"

"Yes."

Adya was silent for a moment. I heard the low shiver of his breath. Then he said, "There were twenty-five hundred Austrian officers among the prisoners when the garrison surrendered."

"He was killed before the surrender. I received a letter from the Ministry of War last summer. He had been leading one of the sorties beyond the fortress walls."

"How do they know? The post wasn't fucking running out of Przemyśl, was it?"

"Were you there?"

"Yes, I was there. We cut telephone cables. We cut telegraph cables."

"We were told that the garrison had managed to send some airmail flights through."

"Thirteen planes in six months. They weren't carrying casualty reports for twenty thousand dead."

"The names of prisoners would've been given to the Red Cross at the transit camp in Kyiv after the surrender."

"Some names. Maybe. If some orderly could be bothered. A hundred and twenty thousand prisoners total. You really think they've got all the names neatly filed in some Red Cross office somewhere?"

**"For the record," Colonel Sosnkowski says to the typist, "I have had it independently confirmed that Rittmeister Emil von Schönborn-Buchheim was killed by enemy fire in an attempted breakout operation on the morning of March nineteenth of last year. Make a note, please, Lieutenant. Continue, Countess."**

"I think," I said to Adya carefully, "I think—even if he were still alive—it would be different. We aren't who we were then. I'm not who was promised to him. He was meant to marry Countess Renata Krystyna Zamoyska. Not Renia, who assists in the surgery for fifty crowns a month."

"And I'm meant to marry Vera Kholodnaya. I saw her on a cinema screen once. He'd be an idiot to call it off. An idiot and a pig."

"I couldn't give him children now," I said softly.

I'd never spoken this aloud until that moment beside Adya in the freezing dark.

I've done my best, as I've said, not to dwell upon that morning in June or the weeks in the hospital afterward. I have my work with Doctor von Brenner in the surgery to occupy my hands and my mind and to salve the hurt in my soul. I carry too much of others' grief to spend time dwelling on my own.

I did pray, for months after Przemyśl fell, that Emi would return safely to me from captivity—and then, even after the letter from the Ministry of War in July, that there could be some mistake, that he could be alive after all. But even if God were to grant this miracle of miracles and send Emi back to me, he could not be mine now.

He was the heir of Schönborn-Buchheim, and he was an only son. He would not marry a woman who could give him no issue. I'm not such a fool as to suppose he would forsake his duty for me. I could be his mistress, perhaps; I could be his kept woman. But I could never be his wife.

"I miscarried—after," I said. "They told me I'll never carry a child to term."

I lay there waiting for Adya's pity or perhaps his disgust. These are, in my experience, the two main reactions to a revelation of this sort. I've heard the whispers around the maternity ward and seen the sidelong looks when a woman comes to us carrying a war child. I was very lucky, one of our nurses told me, to have lost the child so early. I was spared the aspersions upon my virtue, the speculations about my loyalty to the empire and my faithfulness to Emi, that inevitably would've come my way once my condition started to show. I was very lucky that my scars were not visible.

But Adya said, "Why did you stay in Zarudce? Take your fifty crowns and buy a one-way train ticket. Forget this place, forget the war. Go start a life somewhere else. Why are you still here?"

"They need me at the hospital."

He said, "And you, moja pani? What do you need? What do you want?"

You must understand how tired we both were at this point, how muddled in the cold, and how very unlikely it was, given that it had not yet stopped snowing, that either of us would be alive by the time rescue could reach us from Zarudce or from the garrison in Lemberg.

At any rate, I admit that what I wanted most of all, in that moment, was for him to lean a little closer and to say my name rather than *moja pani*.

I had been alone so long. I had gone so long with my own grief and guilt and pain locked away carefully inside me, unseen and unspoken, like a festering wound. It had been so long since I'd heard my name gently on a boy's lips, so long since a boy had touched me because I wanted him to. The only boy who'd ever kissed me, the only boy I ever thought I could love, was dead before the walls of Przemyśl.

And of course you must understand that I believed we would both be dead by morning, and it is a terrible prospect to die alone.

But I said instead, "My own practice. The chance to finish my degree when the war is over, and then my own pediatric practice."

"You'll get it," he said.

I said to him some time later, in the dark and the silence, "Adya."

But he was asleep again, and I was too tired to wake him.

# CHAPTER 18

I woke at dawn the next morning—the first true dawn in three days. There was soft pink daylight slipping into the kitchen through the cracks in the window bricking. I couldn't wake Lieutenant Kijek.

In the latter stages of hypothermia, as I've explained, the victim loses consciousness, the brain being too overwhelmed by the cold to function properly. In truth, I thought he was dead already. My own hands were too numb to feel his pulse or heartbeat.

But I knew better than to take a chance like that. Victims of hypothermia may be dead to all appearances for some time before the heart finally gives out. I am haunted by stories I've heard of mountain climbers left for dead on the Eiger only for it to be determined, in postmortem examinations, that death did not in fact occur until many hours later.

So I undertook to revive the lieutenant with the only means available to me, which was my own body heat. Doctor von Brenner can corroborate, if you need, that direct skin-to-skin contact is most effective in raising a victim's body temperature.

I took off the lieutenant's tunic and undershirt; I opened my coat and apron and blouse and unfastened my various underthings—though, as Captain Baran knows full well, I still had on my chemise and drawers for modesty—and lay down carefully atop him, covering his body with mine, his coat and mine over us.

The lieutenant woke nearly at the same moment that Captain Baran opened the kitchen door. I admit it was very poor timing.

You all know the preceding part of the story better than I, as I didn't have a full picture of that morning until I listened to Captain Baran's testimony. My understanding is that the captain had gone, as usual, to the hospital earlier that morning—this would've been Monday morning now, January third—with the intention of asking me to take coffee with him on the boulevard. It has been his custom on Monday mornings for some time. I have a break from seven to eight o'clock, excepting emergencies, and he routinely comes by and asks me to join him for coffee either at the Hotel Vienna or at the Café de la Paix.

It is my own fault that I never realized this was the captain's attempt to press his suit. I was Mieszko's sister; I thought he felt a sense of obligation for that reason, or perhaps of shared grief. We never spoke of anything personal, beyond some of our memories of Mieszko and our experiences of Vienna.

At any rate, Doctor von Brenner told him at the hospital that I hadn't been in since the snow started, and Captain Baran took it upon himself to organize a cavalry patrol of five riders and look in on me, for which—I wish to be clear—I am very grateful to him.

I did not immediately realize that he was there. The snow in the yard had muffled all hoofbeats and footfalls, and I was so concentrated upon Adya—warming his head and neck and chest under my hands and saying his name over and over, trying to wake him—that I didn't hear the captain open the door.

You can imagine, I'm sure, how it looked from the doorway. It didn't help that when Adya woke just then, confused and still only half conscious, he put his hands on me by reflex, seizing me by the arms and rolling over atop me so that I was pinned to the floor beneath him—a defensive gesture. He had no idea who I was in that moment. He was reacting purely by instinct. And I knew better than to struggle against him—we deal with situations like this quite often in the hospital, and it is never helpful to antagonize a confused, frightened patient any further.

But of course Captain Baran knew none of this and assumed that Adya was hurting me or intending to hurt me. He acted only as he should be expected to act, given that he supposed he was witnessing an assault.

He had, in short order, dragged the lieutenant away from me, thrown him to his knees against the wall, and put the muzzle of his pistol against the lieutenant's head.

I said to him, "Captain, don't."

Captain Baran is no fool. I think he realized he had misread the situation even before I asked him not to shoot. That he immediately misread it again, and just as badly, is quite understandable. Adya and I were both half-dressed, and he had seen my hands on Adya and Adya's hands on me, and he had of course heard me saying Adya's name.

His anger, too, is understandable. It is not simply a spurned lover's jealousy. I am under no illusion that Captain Baran has brought these charges against me only because I've rejected him, or because he cannot stand the thought of another man putting hands on what he considers rightfully his. He deserves more credit than that. He is a loyal servant of the empire—an invaluable member, I understand, of His Highness the Archduke Joseph Ferdinand's staff.

And he was Mieszko's friend. He took Mieszko's death at the Russians' hands very bitterly. It's understandable that he should've been angry at my betrayal. I attribute it to his self-control that he did not execute judgment on me summarily. Plenty of other officers would have.

He said instead, keeping the pistol against Adya's temple and looking off determinedly at the cellar door, "Put your clothes on, Countess."

I said, "Captain." To be completely honest, it didn't occur to me until this moment—as I attempted with some difficulty to close up my corset and blouse while holding Adya's coat around myself with one hand—what it all must look like to him, what he must think he had interrupted.

I was admittedly frightened. Still, I spoke calmly. This is how we're instructed to speak in the hospital so as to maintain order even amidst panic and confusion, and it's a habit I find myself falling back on very often for my own peace of mind. "Captain, this man is suffering from severe hypothermia and frostbite."

"Corporal Pawlik"—this to the junior officer who had tramped in just then; the rest of the troop was with the horses in the yard—"take the countess outside."

Adya had not moved from his knees or spoken. He sat very still, his bare shoulder against the wall. He was conscious enough now to realize that there was a gun against his head.

I said, "Captain Baran, if you please—he requires medical attention."

"He won't very soon."

It is generally useless, in my experience, to appeal to reason against a decision made in anger. It was clear to me that Captain Baran had already determined to shoot the lieutenant and that there was very little I could say to change his mind, no matter how calm or how logical.

But I said, "Captain Baran, he is an unarmed prisoner of war." Which was true, as although he had his pistol still, his five remaining rounds and his knife were both in my own coat pocket, as you'll remember. "And he is protected under the terms of both the Hague Convention and the Stockholm Protocol. He is entitled to medical care."

This was admittedly a bit of embellishment on my part. While the empire is signatory to the Stockholm Protocol as of December, and while the medical corps have been asked to familiarize ourselves with it, we have not yet ratified it. It made no difference to Captain Baran in any case.

"Corporal," he repeated, ignoring me very deliberately, "take the countess outside."

I said, "Franek, please—for my sake."

If it's useless to appeal to reason in a situation such as this, it's downright dangerous to appeal to emotion. The captain had, to this point, been making a very great effort to contain himself and to conduct himself professionally despite his anger. He had been careful so far not to look either at me or at Adya but fixedly at the cellar door. But he looked at me now.

"For your sake, Countess? For *your* sake? Six months and you won't deign to give me so much as a kiss, and now suddenly it's 'For my sake, please, Franek'? For this Muscovite filth?"

You see how a man gets mistaken ideas when a woman puts herself in his debt.

That poor young corporal had frozen in the doorway. This was above his grade, as they say.

I said to Captain Baran, "I'll do anything you want, Franek. I'll give you anything you want."

At this, Adya made a sudden, foolish attempt to clamber up off his knees. The captain turned the pistol in his hand and smashed the butt swiftly and viciously across Adya's face—and then again, and again, and again, until Adya had crumpled senseless to the floor, his face awash in blood. It all happened very quickly.

The captain holstered his pistol. His face was stark white, but his voice was very calm. "No self-respecting gentleman will ever want anything from you, Countess. No self-respecting gentleman wants damaged goods."

He snapped some order to the corporal after that; they put me on one of the horses. I didn't tell them about my broken rib.

I don't know what they did with Lieutenant Kijek. Only three of us made that ride back to Lemberg, so I presume the other three of Captain Baran's men remained with him until an ambulance cart could be sent out.

That was the last I saw of him until I saw him brought into the courtroom this morning. But I knew he must be alive because they told me—when they told me the charges—that this tribunal would be sentencing both of us. Me for "actions deemed disruptive to the war effort" and him for espionage.

It seems you were more immediately suspicious of his story than I was.

# CHAPTER 19

The typist finishes.

He pulls a lever and turns a knob and discreetly flexes his fingers below the edge of his desk. His paper waits ready on a new line. The parlor is silent, save for a muffled cough and the protesting creak of a chair as someone shifts his weight and the gentle scratch of Colonel Sosnkowski's pen. He's writing out something for Commandant Piłsudski on a piece of notepaper.

He says to me, still writing, "Is there anything else, Countess?"

I remind him, "It was you who asked for my account, Colonel. It falls to you to say whether I've answered satisfactorily."

One of General von Linsingen's subordinates, a senior officer, an Oberst judging by the insignia on his collar and shoulder boards, says, "Get on with it, Colonel. We've wasted enough time here."

"By your leave, then, Countess," Colonel Sosnkowski says mildly, "I believe you've given us everything we need. We will proceed to your sentencing."

He lays his pen down. They confer just for a moment, he

and Commandant Piłsudski, their heads bent together over the table, their voices low. Commandant Piłsudski speaks in turn to General von Linsingen, who gives him a curt, wordless nod.

Commandant Piłsudski clears his throat and declares stiffly in German, "Countess Renata Krystyna Zamoyska is found guilty of disrupting the war effort of the Austro-Hungarian state, in violation of Section Sixty-Seven of the Criminal Code. The sentence is death, to be carried out immediately by firing squad."

At the back of the room, Lieutenant Kijek, who doesn't speak German but who presumably knows the word *tod*, leaps up, unbalanced slightly by his bound hands, practically kicking his chair out of the way, and the two soldiers who've sat flanking him all morning haul him back down again roughly by the arms.

Everything goes very quickly now.

Colonel Sosnkowski says to me, "Do you have any requests, Countess?"

I draw a careful breath. "Yes—if you please, Colonel. My priest is Father Urban. I would like to see him first."

"My apologies, Countess." Colonel Sosnkowski's voice is gentle. "We won't have time to summon him from Zarudce. The road is still impassable by car. The troop chaplain is here if you would like to see him—Father Teodor."

"Yes, thank you."

He nods. "It will be arranged."

"And my mother has kin in England. I believe their name is Wimsey, in Norfolk. I would like to make sure that they are notified of her death and her burial place. It was of course out of the question to write them at the time."

Colonel Sosnkowski makes another note on his paper. "I'll see to it personally, Countess."

"Thank you, Colonel. You've been very kind."

I have nothing else to ask. I am resolved not to bring any further shame upon the name Zamoyski by asking to be buried with my mother and Mieszko, both of whom died with their honor intact. I pray only that their memory will be unsullied by mine.

I have nothing to bequeath—the manor and grounds and the rowhouse on Marka Street in Lemberg will go to the Austro-Hungarian crown upon my death—and no one to receive a bequest. My father's line of the family ended with Mieszko. My mother's kin in England, the offspring of a great-aunt I never knew, are as distant to me as strangers.

My affairs are very tidy. I will ask Father Teodor to pass a message to Father Urban concerning that parcel of Pani Adamczyk's, which, as far as I know, still sits on my kitchen counter where I left it when I returned Leo's pocket watch. Since I cannot do it myself, I would like Father Urban to be the one bearing the news of Leo's death to his widowed mother. He is wise and sensitive in such matters—he has certainly been a solace to me.

Colonel Sosnkowski stands and bows to me very courteously. None of the rest bother. General von Linsingen beckons for an orderly to bring a fresh teapot. His officers are all drumming restless fingers, tapping booted heels, tipping their chairs absently back and forth, impatient to move on to Lieutenant Kijek's trial—understandably so. My testimony, which has taken up the better part of their morning, does not ultimately mean all that much.

And I think everyone here is relieved to be back on terra cognita, as it were. The business of examining a male prisoner of war will be more familiar to them and therefore perhaps less discomfiting, less embarrassing, than dealing with me.

The lieutenant's guards are already hurrying him past me to the front of the room, forcing his head down so that I have no chance to speak with him or even to meet his eye as he passes. My own guards are waiting for me at the parlor doors.

It is over. Or, at least, it is out of my hands. My part is done. Mieszko will be proud and, I hope, able to rest easier. To be honest, that is all I wanted.

I would've liked, though, to say goodbye to Lieutenant Kijek. I doubt I'll have another chance, and it feels odd, after all we've endured together, to part without a word.

But of course that is the nature of this line of work. I expect he knows that as well as I.

# CHAPTER 20

The quiet knock at my cell door, half an hour or so later, is not the promised Father Teodor but rather Colonel Sosnkowski himself.

He wouldn't have had to leave the house to reach my cell from the parlor, and yet he's wearing coat and hat and scarf, being careful to obscure his face. He looks around critically as he takes off his various layers of outerwear.

My cell is not unpleasant. It's clean and dry and quite warm, being so close to the kitchen, and I have a camp bed and a little table with a chair, and though there's no window, there is an electric light, which I can switch on and off at my convenience. It's certainly much better appointed than a pile of old feed sacks in the corner of my kitchen. But Colonel Sosnkowski says, with obvious distaste, "I apologize, Countess, that this has been necessary."

"I've been quite comfortable, Colonel."

"May I?" He locks the door. We sit at the little table. He takes the chair, and I perch on the edge of my cot, and he lays his briefcase on the table between us. His every movement is deliberate.

There is a certain cool, graceful precision about him that I imagine is lethal in action.

I've never met him in the flesh before this morning. I didn't know him by sight, unlike Commandant Piłsudski with his dramatic moustache; I hadn't the slightest idea who he was until he was introduced as my examiner. But I did know his name already, both his real name and his code name, Szef, "Chief," which was how he was always addressed in the dispatches. And I knew he was Mieszko's immediate superior within the Organizacja Wojskowa—and the source of Mieszko's orders.

"You'll have to forgive us the theatrics," Colonel Sosnkowski says to me as he opens his briefcase. "Kijek has spent four days in German custody, which has made things difficult. Obviously, we couldn't demand his release on the grounds that he's one of our intelligence agents. They did finally agree to let us handle the questioning, provided it was done in German . . . and you'll excuse me, Countess, for insisting upon pulling at every last thread of your testimony, painful as it must have been. I was quite simply trying to kill some time. General von Linsingen and his staff have now left for Kowel and won't be able to observe the executions—which, as you can imagine, simplifies things for us a great deal. It isn't technically difficult to fake an execution by firing squad, but it's always risky. Of course, it's much more difficult to fake a hanging, which is one of the reasons we were so keen to have you tried before a military court."

I say slowly, "The executions will be faked?" I've spent so long now preparing myself for my death that I'm caught rather off guard by the prospect of absolution.

Colonel Sosnkowski looks startled. "I apologize, Countess," he says again. "I thought that was clear. When they told you that the commandant and I would be hearing your case—"

"I wasn't sure whether I had succeeded in convincing Commandant Piłsudski of my loyalties."

He is silent for a moment, giving this the same serious, patient consideration that he seems to give everything. "Ah. Because you said you would've saved Kijek's life regardless of whether you knew he was Polish—regardless, presumably, of whether you knew he was one of my operatives. Is that why?"

"Yes."

"I would like to think," he says, "that there is room for compassion in our Poland. I would certainly like to think that there is room for honesty." He hesitates. "With that in mind, Countess . . . before we go any further, I'd like to give you an explanation regarding the circumstances of your brother's death. It's clear that the Russian command had come to realize that Lieutenant Zamoyski was, in fact, using his position to pass intelligence to us from inside the occupied territories. It's clear that he was killed on General Brusilov's orders after all, despite the earlier clemency."

"Yes."

"We had a breach—a Russian agent in our own ranks. He had access to the identities of several of our agents behind Russian lines. He has been caught and dealt with. I regret that this was not done in time to save your brother's life. Lieutenant Zamoyski was one of my very best. You know, perhaps, that he was with me on a number of operations in Privislinsky Krai before the war."

"Yes. He always spoke very highly of you, Colonel."

"I was very glad to learn, Countess, that you were alive." His voice is quiet. "It is to my own great shame that you've had to endure the public indignity of this trial on top of everything else."

"I knew the risks involved, Colonel, as did Mieszko."

"Nevertheless," he says, "I speak for both the commandant and myself in offering my apologies and my gratitude, insufficient as they are." He lays an envelope on the table. "With your permission, Countess, I'd like to ask you a few questions—routine questions. I like to keep all my loose ends tied up, as I'm sure you can understand."

"Yes, Colonel."

"When did Kijek reveal to you that he was, in fact, an agent of the Organizacja Wojskowa?"

"After Captain Witkowski's death—that afternoon. He told me that he had come to Zarudce hoping to find Mieszko, who had been his contact when he was stationed in Lemberg during the occupation. He was trying to arrange for Captain Witkowski's safe passage to Petrograd, and he brought the boy to Zarudce because he thought Mieszko might be able to help him. He hadn't yet heard that Mieszko was dead."

"Presumably, young Witkowski did not know that Kijek was one of our agents."

"Presumably not, or Lieutenant Kijek wouldn't have deemed it necessary to wait until he was dead to speak to me about it."

"Did it strike you that Kijek was jeopardizing his mission and your brother's for Captain Witkowski's sake?"

"Lieutenant Kijek's mission would also have been jeopardized had he been executed by the Russian command at Rovno for insubordination in the matter of Łąka. We may thank Captain Witkowski that he was not."

Colonel Sosnkowski nods; the answer is satisfactory. "How much of his mission did Kijek reveal to you?"

I hesitate. I have no wish to bring any more trouble upon

Lieutenant Kijek. He told me much more than he should have, I imagine, given that I am not myself technically an agent of the Organizacja Wojskowa—only a courier, recruited not for my skill or qualifications but merely out of urgent necessity.

"I knew a great deal about the parameters of the mission already, Colonel. During the occupation, I was the one picking up Lieutenant Kijek's dispatches from the cache in Lemberg each week and delivering them to Mieszko—because of course his cover was that he was convalescing at home. I knew the contact must be an officer in the Russian army. Lieutenant Kijek told me that he'd first met Mieszko in Lublin two years ago, just before the war—the lieutenant helped supply weapons for one of your operations in Privislinsky Krai. They met again in Lemberg after the city fell, at which point Mieszko recruited the lieutenant as an agent of the Organizacja within the Russians' Nineteenth Infantry Division."

"Did Kijek say anything to you of the mission's objective?"

"No, Colonel. Neither he nor Mieszko."

Not a lie, but Colonel Sosnkowski's ear is too well attuned by now to my half-truths. His gaze is sharp and thoughtful. "But you knew the objective."

"I guessed, Colonel. I didn't know."

"Tell me."

"With respect, Colonel. Lieutenant Kijek is an ethnic Pole, a commoner, with a battlefield commission. His opportunities for advancing any further through the Russian ranks are quite limited. You would not have targeted the lieutenant for recruitment if your objective was to place an agent within General Brusilov's headquarters or on his staff. But the lieutenant would be ideally placed to reach Polish conscripts among General Brusilov's enlisted men and to gauge the temperament toward uprising—perhaps to help organize it when the time comes."

Colonel Sosnkowski is silent. Then he says, "You make a formidable opponent, Countess Zamoyska."

"We are not opponents."

"No. The opposite, I hope. I should inform you that the commandant has authorized me to offer you a commission. You would hold your brother's rank and pay grade. You would report to me, as he did. We would need to place you somewhere other than Lemberg for the time being, but it needn't be too far afield—unless, of course, you wish it to be. Your fluency in both German and Russian leaves several doors open to you."

I say carefully, "I thank you, Colonel, but I think I am better suited to serve our Poland in other capacities. This was Mieszko's work, not mine."

"You'll have to leave Lemberg in any case, Countess."

"Yes. I'm prepared to do so."

He nods, his face blank. It is, I think, the answer he was expecting. He pushes the envelope to me across the table. "My second offer, then," he says.

The letter within is written in German on heavy, good-quality cream-colored stationery of a sort I've not seen since before the war. The seal in blue ink on the letterhead is that of the Medical Faculty of the University of Vienna.

It is an acceptance letter.

The name is not mine, of course. It cannot be, as Countess Renata Krystyna Zamoyska has by now been executed by firing squad. The letter is made out instead to Renata Czartoryska, as is the travel permit tucked beneath. A smaller second envelope holds forty-five hundred crowns in banknotes. It takes me a little while to count through them all.

"There is a ticket waiting for you at the central station," Colonel Sosnkowski tells me quietly. "The nine o'clock train through Budapest, tonight. The money is yours. It was your brother's. Nine months' worth of back pay, September of 1914 through June of last year—his salary through the occupation. It should've been paid to you months ago."

I fold the letter back up very slowly. If not for the weight of the paper, I think I would have a hard time believing it was real. I hold it on my lap and say to him, "How? How did you get this?"

He smiles.

"This is my work, Countess," he says, "not yours."

# CHAPTER 21

Beyond seven mountains, beyond seven forests, there was a beautiful princess imprisoned in an enchanted castle atop a hill of pure crystal glass.

The glass slopes were so slick and sheer that no one had ever managed to reach the top and rescue her, though many had tried—the best and bravest knights from all the world over. Each and every one of them had slipped and plummeted to his death, so that the foot of the hill had slowly become a hideous graveyard littered with old bones and the decaying corpses of men and horses and the rusted, battered scraps of once-fine armor.

After seven long years of this, a poor farm boy, bereft of anything and anyone in the world, determined that he would make the climb, since he had nothing to lose. He had no fine horse or armor, but he had his resourcefulness and his courage. He killed a lynx in the forest and used its sharp claws to scratch handholds and footholds into the steep glass hillside. In this manner, he made it farther than any of the knights who had come before him. He had very nearly reached the top, when suddenly a giant eagle rose up and flew at him, tearing into him with its fearsome talons.

The pain was immense, but he took hold of the eagle and wouldn't let it go until it had carried him the rest of the way to the hilltop. There, he cut off the eagle's talons with his pocket-knife and dropped right into the castle garden. The princess healed his wounds with the peels of the magical golden apples that grew there.

That was the secret, of course—that you had to be willing to endure the pain of the eagle's talons. There was no other way to reach the hilltop. That was the lesson of the story as my father told it. And of course that story ends as all those stories end, with a marriage and a wedding feast and all the dead brought magically back to life, restored by the dying eagle's shed blood as it falls to earth.

That story always seemed to me more bittersweet than anything else. Yes, they're happy together, the boy and the princess. They want for nothing. But—if you really think about it—they can never leave that hilltop, can they? They can never go home. They're doomed to live out their days alone in their enchanted castle, watching the world below go on without them. The only way off the hill is in the eagle's talons. And they killed the eagle.

But then I think, no—the story doesn't end there.

How can it? The farm boy was clever and brave enough to reach the hilltop when everyone before him had failed. The princess was patient and steadfast enough to endure seven years of dashed hopes without giving in to despair. They trust each other, they care for each other. They make each other strong.

They'll find a way off that hilltop. They'll find a way home.

I am free—and yet not really free.

I am not sure I will ever be really free. Perhaps if Commandant Piłsudski and Colonel Sosnkowski succeed, if our dream of independent Poland becomes real after all . . . perhaps then we will be able to speak aloud of all we've done in this war.

Perhaps I will be able at last to inscribe it upon my beloved Mieszko's headstone: that he gave his life unflinchingly on the twenty-first of June, 1915—Colonel Sosnkowski has confirmed the date for me—in the service of a country that had not yet been born.

Perhaps I will be able to use my own name again. Of course I don't much care about my title anymore; it seems very clear that the world in which such things mattered is in its last bloody death throes and will soon be gone forever. But there is still a part of me, unrepentantly proud, that wishes people to know that Renata Krystyna Zamoyska was not in fact a coward or a traitor. That she too was a patriot, that she too was brave.

Perhaps one day the wounds of war will all be healed, and the apple trees will be in blossom again on the hill above the garden, and I will be free to come home.

One of Commandant Piłsudski's orderlies—himself an agent of the Organizacja, I presume, and privy to the deception—drives me into the city. Colonel Sosnkowski has paid for a room for me at the Hotel Astoria on Gródecka Street, just down from the central station, where I may wait for the nine o'clock train.

At the concierge's desk, I give my name as Renata Czartoryska. My own dress is folded away with a change of underthings in my bag, where it will remain until Lemberg is safely behind me. I wear a borrowed nurse's uniform that Colonel Sosnkowski has procured for me: plain dress of light-blue wool, apron and wimple of white cotton, rather like a novice's habit. The dress is too short about the ankles and too high about the waist; I've always been taller than most girls my age.

Name and uniform are both so clearly ill fitting, so clearly not mine, that I think surely the concierge must notice—surely he must see through the lie—surely all our work is about to come undone. But he simply takes down the name that is not mine and directs the porter where to take my bag.

I've forgotten small luxuries. I don't remember the last time I sat down on a real bed, complete with box spring and mattress and soft feather bolsters and crisp, clean white sheets. I don't remember the last time I drew steaming hot water straight from a faucet. There is a telephone on the desk; there is a gas heater on the wall. There are scented French soaps on the washstand in the bathroom—rose and lilac and lavender, wrapped in tissue paper stamped with fleurs-de-lis. There are Swiss chocolates in gold foil on the bedside table.

I wouldn't have thought twice about any of these things before the war. But now—

I can't stand to be in this room. I can't stand to pretend things can just go back.

I draw a bath into the giant claw-foot tub—I do need one very badly. I dry my hair at the dressing table and braid it. I put on my clean underthings and the nurse's uniform.

In the lobby, the concierge summons a taxicab for me. It is just now six o'clock in the evening, but there will be a line at the ticketing window later—there is always a line at departure—and I don't want to risk missing the train. I believe the service to Vienna runs only twice per day now, once in the morning via Kraków and once in the evening via Budapest, and I don't want to wait until morning. I'll pick up my ticket and perhaps find something to eat at one of the station cafés or at one of the street vendors' booths in the park. I doubt I can stand the hotel restaurant any more than I can stand my room.

I spot Lieutenant Kijek from the ticketing window.

The ticketing agent, a tiny old man who speaks to me in lovely Austrian-tinged German, is taking very great care to explain to me that I'll need to make two transfers, the first at Przemyśl, the second at Budapest Keleti, and I'll need to show my ticket and travel permit for each, and though it will be difficult to miss the Budapest transfer because it's a terminal, I'll need to be paying close attention so as not to miss the stop at Przemyśl, especially as this transfer will happen very early in the morning . . .

And there he is, standing on the far platform across the tracks, leaning a shoulder on one of the wrought iron pillars supporting the train shed.

He's wearing civilian clothes: drab gray coat and cap as foreign and ill fitted to him as this nurse's uniform is to me. He has no bag. He holds a cigarette in one hand—foolishly. His hands remain blistered with frostbite, and he still has no gloves. His free hand, at least, is stuck in his coat pocket. He doesn't see me. He's looking away down the empty track into the dark.

For a moment, I wonder: Is he here because he, too, wishes he could've had the chance to say goodbye?

But no. Of course not. He couldn't have known that I would be here. Certainly not that I would be here now, when the service to Vienna doesn't leave for nearly another three hours.

The service to Lublin stops at the far platform in seven minutes. He is here, like me, to catch a train.

His Lublin is liberated now. Privislinsky Krai, the Russian-ruled Vistula Land in which he grew up, no longer exists as of this past September, when the German offensive swept through all the way to Vilna. Of course when we speak of someplace like Lublin being "liberated," we mean only that it is no longer under Russian occupation. There is not really much difference between groveling to the kaiser and groveling to the tsar—he was right. It is not really liberation to trade one occupation for another.

So I suppose he, like me, like every Pole, is free without really being free. I suppose none of us can really go home.

But perhaps one day.

I have his knife and his cartridges in my coat pocket still. Nobody ever took them from me. Nobody searched me bodily. One more thing for which I may truly thank Captain Baran, who prevented his men from doing so.

The knife is not a kit knife or a trench knife—it isn't standard issue. It is, I think, something personal, though there's no inscription. The haft is sleek, dark walnut wood worn down soft and supple from long use, etched inexpertly but lovingly with an intertwining pattern of leafy vines and flowers and unidentifiable birds. I should've asked Colonel Sosnkowski to return it to Lieutenant Kijek. It was careless of me to forget.

I thank the ticketing agent and cross the subway to the far platform.

The platform is very nearly empty apart from the two of us. This is not the last train for Lublin tonight. There's another at eight o'clock that I presume will be much more crowded. He doesn't look at me as I come up the subway steps, other than briefly to note the nurse's uniform. He turns his head away very properly.

He doesn't recognize me.

It is not, I think, just a matter of the nurse's uniform. He has of course only ever seen me by gray half-light or by feeble lamplight. He has only ever seen me dirty and exhausted, and only when he was himself exhausted. Even at the Potocki manor, he never got a proper look at my face, being seated behind me during the trial. We are two strangers.

I hesitate before I speak to him. Following strict protocol, I suppose I shouldn't use his name or reveal that I know him, even if "Adrian Kijek" is not in fact his real name. But we're alone, and the Lublin train is pulling in—I can see the headlamp moving steadily nearer up the track in the dark—and I will never have this chance again because I will never see him again.

I say to him, "Adrian."

He turns his head to take me in now, lingering on my face. He runs a swift, sharp glance around the perimeter of the train shed as though to make sure no one is watching. He straightens against the pillar, putting out his cigarette, exhaling a last soft cloud of smoke through his nostrils. He returns the stub frugally to the packet inside the breast of his coat. His face is guarded. His shoulders are very straight.

"Moja pani," he says.

"Here. I wanted to give this back to you."

He looks at the knife on my outstretched palm. He makes no move to take it.

"It's yours," I prompt him. "I took it—do you remember? It was in my coat pocket."

He hisses a breath. "It isn't mine. I took it off a sentry when we broke out of the holding camp, same as the pistol. Do you think they would've let me keep that on me in the camp?"

"Take it. Perhaps you can sell it to Rewolucyjni Mściciele."

He hesitates. Then he takes it. He is careful not to let his hand touch mine. His fingers are angrily red, scabbed with burst blisters.

"You need gloves," I say to him.

He shrugs. "I had five crowns left after the ticket. I could buy gloves, or I could buy cigarettes. So."

"You paid the fare?"

Another hissed breath. "I've hopped trains, but not in January, and not for two hundred kilometers."

"No—I meant Szef should've paid the fare for you. He paid mine. Have they paid you anything?"

He is watching the engine draw up slowly to the platform. He doesn't answer.

"Adya, have they paid you anything?" I repeat.

"They paid me."

"Ten crowns? Enough for a railway ticket and a packet of cigarettes?"

"Fifteen hundred crowns. I paid three hundred to some fucking—some Germans to tell me where they buried Vitya. Some unmarked hole in the ground. Twelve hundred for them to put him in Łyczakowski under a gravestone. Pickpocketed ten back from one of them. Ticket and cigarettes."

"It was good of you," I say gently.

"Should've just let them put a bullet in my head in Rovno. That would've been good of me. Would've solved everything."

He's tense and angry and embarrassed. He's close enough that I can feel it.

He says, "Forgive me, moja pani."

I say, "The commandant's orderly told me it's possible that Captain Baran may be brought up on charges over his conduct. I thought you'd like to know."

"That kurwa."

"Though he said any charges would be difficult to prosecute, given—"

"That you and I are dead."

"He was Mieszko's friend," I say after a moment. "I try to remember that. I try to understand. They were at the war college together. Most of the other officer candidates came from old noble families, and he didn't—you understand. But Mieszko didn't care. He could make a friend of anyone."

"Your brother," Adya says, "was a much better man than I am."

"He was always very brave. Sometimes foolishly so."

"He was the second-bravest person I've ever known," Adya says.

The train comes very slowly to a halt before us, coughing steam and hissing like the Wawel dragon. We stand there together, side by side, as the Lemberg passengers spill from the cars.

I ask him, "Will you keep working for Szef in Lublin?"—even though I know that he can't answer me, or that I can't believe him if he does. "Has he asked you to keep working?"

"No. They're done with me. No use for me out of a Russian uniform. I didn't go to the war college." His voice is sour. He lets out a breath. His shoulders drop. He looks at me; his face softens. "And you? Where are you going?"

"Vienna"—even though I'm not sure I'm allowed to tell him.

"For him?"

"No, to the university. They've paid my tuition at the medical university."

He nods. "Good."

The crowd clears slowly. The train guard is making his way from car to car down the length of the platform. The porters are putting aboard the last of the new luggage. The driver is leaning his head out of the engine window, awaiting the guard's whistle.

Adya says, "It was good to see you again, moja pani."

I say to him, "Adya."

He has already taken a step toward the train. He hesitates now; he looks back.

I say to him, "I wanted you to kiss me."

He says nothing. He looks at me.

"That night, when you asked me what I wanted—do you remember? I wanted you to kiss me."

He is silent as though absorbing this. Then he says, his voice very low and careful, "And if I asked you tonight, moja pani?"

"I want you to kiss me."

He steps close again. I can hear the hitch in his breath. He tilts his head as though to study me. His lips touch my cheek, then the corner of my mouth, then my lips, cautious as a whisper. I close my eyes, and his callused thumbs brush over my shut eyelids; his hands slip around to cradle my head. His mouth moves gently over mine. When I part my lips to draw a breath, I can taste him—salt and smoke and tobacco-sweetness.

He is still kissing me when the whistle sounds. He is still kissing me when the train pulls away. His arms are about me, holding me close, and he is murmuring something low and soft and warm against my lips between each kiss. It takes me a moment, over the thud of my heart, to realize he is murmuring my name.

❖❖❖❖

I lay my ticket on the counter at the ticketing window.

"If you please—I'd like to exchange this for a double compartment."

"For the nine o'clock to Vienna?"

"Yes."

"You'll need to make two transfers," the ticketing agent says, "first at Przemyśl, then at Budapest Keleti. And you must be careful not to miss Przemyśl . . ."

# POSTLUDE

## SATURDAY, MARCH 3, 1917
## VIENNA, AUSTRIA

Our apartment is in Brigittenau, between the Augarten and the canal. It's small and quite modest—one room above a little wineshop on the Jägerstrasse, let to us by the war widow who owns the shop. We have a kitchen table and two chairs and a bed, all of which Adya made by hand with pieces of scrap wood from the freight yard at the Nordwestbahnhof; he's hunting the wood for my bookshelf next. There are young narcissuses blooming in the window box above the sink, ruffled white heads bent to catch the bright spring sunlight; there are dried heather sprigs in a green glass bottle on our table. Our bedspread is cheery checkered patchwork, light-blue wool and white cotton. I sewed it from the nurse's uniform I wore leaving Lemberg more than a year ago.

We have no need of anything more. We have enough, with Adya's income from the freight yard and what's left of Mieszko's back pay, to make a good life until I finish my course of study at the university.

The war is a distant thought here in the imperial capital. An item of some vague interest in the newspaper. A topic for debate over chess in the park, under the blossoming apricot trees. There are worsening shortages of flour and sugar and milk and coffee, yes, and if one wishes to have fresh fruits and vegetables one must grow one's own. But the people here have never heard the thunder of artillery fire or seen an occupying army march down the Ringstrasse. For the most part, except when the hospital trains bring convalescent wounded from the front, the city feels much the same as it felt three years ago. In fact, I feel sometimes as though I myself am slipping back slowly into that old life. Except . . .

A funny thing happened last night. Or not funny, I suppose, as it stung very much at the time, but certainly ironic.

I was attending a dinner given by Doctor Hauptner, chair of the pediatrics faculty—it's his custom to give a dinner at the Ofenloch for his faculty and students at the beginning of the term. After my first one, last March, I haven't made Adya come with me; I know these sorts of things make him uncomfortable, especially as his German is still rather limited apart from cursing.

But anyway, who else should have been dining there at the Ofenloch last night but His Excellency the elder Graf von Schönborn-Buchheim, Emi's father?

He's evidently acquainted with Doctor Hauptner—my understanding is that he made rather a generous endowment to the university at some point or other—and Doctor Hauptner made introductions all around the table, and the Graf von Schönborn-Buchheim did not recognize me.

Of course he hadn't seen me since we met that once in person three years ago, when I was his guest at Göllersdorf, though we had exchanged written condolences that July after Emi's death. And of course I am not going by my full name and title anymore. Doctor Hauptner introduced me as he knows me, as Renata Kijek, Pani Kijek. The Graf took my hand, bowed over it, kissed it, and smiled at me very politely and properly, without the faintest idea that once upon a time, beyond seven mountains, beyond seven forests, I was to have been his daughter-in-law.

In that moment, I was keenly aware of my life as it might have been, and my life as it is.

I excused myself from the dinner early. Vienna nights are still quite cool in March, but I walked over to the lamplit Volksgarten and stood there on the edge of the Ringstrasse where Emi had kissed me in the limousine three years ago, and I said goodbye to him for the last time, aloud into the dark.

Then I crossed the canal back to the little apartment in Brigittenau, where my future was waiting for me.

# AUTHOR'S NOTE

This story began with a single photograph.

A few years ago, historian and archivist Nicolai Eberholst, who runs a social media account (@PikeGrey1418) dedicated to the history of World War I's Eastern Front, posted a photo taken in July of 1915, in the Austro-Hungarian-ruled region of Galicia. It shows two Austro-Hungarian soldiers guarding a young Ukrainian peasant boy, probably in his early teens, who has been accused of spying for the Russians and sentenced to death.

The photo is rightfully disturbing, perhaps all the more so when you consider that this sort of thing wasn't unusual in that place at that time—the Austro-Hungarian authorities clearly had no qualms about documenting it on film. Both sides, Central and Allied, committed atrocities against civilian populations on the Eastern Front on a massive scale. Deportations, summary executions, and massacres were commonplace. Civilian death tolls on the Eastern Front from the years 1914–1918 are impossible to tally exactly but are staggering by any estimation. According to *Britannica*, approximately two million civilians of the Russian Empire were casualties of war; half a million of them were Poles or Lithuanians. Approximately three hundred thousand civilians of Austria-Hungary died, the majority of them Poles. (These numbers do not include military deaths on the Eastern Front, which themselves number in the several millions.)

It's far too easy to lose sight of a single tragedy against a backdrop of millions of tragedies, but that photograph stayed with me. I wondered about that boy. I wondered about the people around him and how they might have reacted to his death. Would they have viewed it with indifference? Would they perhaps have considered it justified? Would anyone have tried to defend him?

Renata was my way to answer these questions. Her story ultimately went in a direction I didn't expect—I had no idea about the final twist until Colonel Sosnkowski knocked on her cell door. But it started with that photograph.

Poland did not exist as a sovereign state during World War I, despite a long and proud history. Control of its territory had been divided up among Russia, Prussia, and Austria-Hungary at the end of the eighteenth century. In the Russian partition—called variously the Kingdom of Poland, Congress Poland, Russian Poland, or the Vistula Land (Privislinsky Krai in Russian)—the tsarist authorities adopted increasingly harsh measures to stamp out Polish nationalism, particularly following uprisings in 1830 and 1863. The use of the Polish language was forbidden; books of Polish literature and history were banned; ethnic Poles were shut out from positions in government and academia.

Many Poles became involved in underground resistance against Russian rule in the years leading up to World War I. Among them were Józef Piłsudski and Kazimierz Sosnkowski. After the outbreak of war in 1914, they worked with the Austro-Hungarian authorities to create a distinctly Polish armed force to fight the Russians: the Polish Legions. Piłsudski became commander of the First Brigade of the Legions. Sosnkowski served as his chief of staff. Their allegiance to the Central Powers was always second to their goal of reestablishing an independent Poland; both were imprisoned by the Germans in 1917 for refusing to swear an oath of loyalty to the German Empire and were only freed on November 8, 1918, when Germany's collapse was imminent. Three days later, on November 11—Armistice Day—Poland formally declared its independence. Józef Piłsudski was named commander in chief and given the task of forming a new national government.

The so-called Second Polish Republic lasted only twenty-one years, until Poland fell to the Germans and Soviets in 1939. But Piłsudski, who died in 1935, continues to be regarded as the founder of the modern Polish state. Kazimierz Sosnkowski, meanwhile, had a distinguished military career that continued through the Second World War. Unable to return to communist-controlled Poland after the war, he died in Canada in 1969.

For a nuanced treatment of both men and their complicated legacies, I recommend Joshua D. Zimmerman's biography of Piłsudski (*Jozef Pilsudski: Founding Father of Modern Poland*). I also benefited greatly from Matthew Raymond Schwonek's dissertation on Sosnkowski (*Kazimierz Sosnkowski, the Polish Army, and Polish State-Building, 1905–1944*), which details the many disparate parts—among them the Organizacja Wojskowa—that together made up the Polish independence movement.

For a general history of this theater of World War I, I recommend Nick Lloyd's *The Eastern Front: A History of the Great War 1914–1918*. For a more singularly focused history, Alexander Watson's *The Fortress: The Siege of Przemyśl and the Making of Europe's Bloodlands* proved an invaluable resource.

# QUESTIONS FOR DISCUSSION

1. At the beginning of the story, before you know much about Renia, what can you tell about her personality from the way she speaks to her examiners at her trial?

2. Of the various reasons Renia gives for turning "traitor," which do you find the most compelling and why?

3. How has Renia's status as a noblewoman shielded her from certain wartime hardships? In what ways has that status not protected her?

4. Which of Renia's skills did you find most surprising or interesting, and why? What drove her to develop that skill?

5. How are Renia's actions guided by her feelings about her home and her family? Pick one decision she makes and trace it back to the influence of her mother, her father, or her brother.

6. How has her assault in June affected Renia in both practical and emotional terms?

7. Renia and Adya don't spend much time getting to know each other in a conventional sense. How do they learn about each other through actions over the course of the three days they spend together?

8. How is Renia's relationship with Emi different from the one she develops with Adya? What are some key differences between Emi and Adya, and what might they have in common?

9. How does Renia use folktales to contextualize her life and signal her deeper emotions to the reader?

10. How does the narrative build tension even as it gives away certain outcomes? At what part of the story were you in the most suspense about what would happen next? What part surprised you most?

# ACKNOWLEDGMENTS

Thank you, as always, to my critique partners, Erin Litteken and Marina Scott, and to my other early readers: Elizabeth McCrina, Marte Mittet, Kaye Acosta, and Leah Good.

Thank you to Dr. hab. Mateusz Świetlicki for reading multiple drafts and helping me with my Polish grammar and vocabulary. Any mistakes are most certainly my own.

Thank you to my readers—and to the booksellers, librarians, and educators who help get my books into readers' hands.

Thank you to my agent, Jennie Kendrick, for her steadfast guidance through the ups and downs of the writerly life.

Thank you to copyeditor Heidi Mann, designer Kim Morales, map artist Laura K. Westlund, and the entire team at Lerner/Carolrhoda Lab.

Thank you to my editor, Amy Fitzgerald, for letting me write such a very Polish book and for shaping and strengthening the story so skillfully.

And thank you to the whole McCrina clan, for being my first and dearest supporters.

# ABOUT THE AUTHOR

Amanda McCrina is a writer, historian, and bookseller. She holds a degree in history and political science from the University of West Georgia. Her YA novels include *Traitor*, *The Silent Unseen*, and *I'll Tell You No Lies*. She lives outside Nashville, Tennessee.